A CORNISH VENGEANCE

Silas Venning, millionaire owner of a luxury yacht company, is found hanged in a remote Cornish wood. It looks like suicide — but his widow, celebrated artist Laura Anstey, doesn't think so. She enlists Loveday Ross to help prove her suspicions. But there can be no doubts about the killing of Venning's former employee Brian Penrose — not when he's mown down by a hit-and-run driver right in front of Loveday's boyfriend, DI Sam Kitto. Could they be dealing with *two* murders?

RENA GEORGE

A CORNISH VENGEANCE

Complete and Unabridged

LINFORD
Leicester

First published in Great Britain

First Linford Edition
published 2016

*A catalogue record for this book is available
from the British Library.*

ISBN 978–1–4448–2951–8

Published by
F. A. Thorpe (Publishing)
Anstey, Leicestershire

Set by Words & Graphics Ltd.
Anstey, Leicestershire
Printed and bound in Great Britain by
T. J. International Ltd., Padstow, Cornwall

This book is printed on acid-free paper

1

Loveday divided the scrambled eggs between two slices of slightly burned toast and turned to Sam. 'Are you sure it was suicide?'

He looked up, narrowing his eyes at her. 'Why?'

She shrugged. 'Not sure. Just seems odd, that's all. Silas Venning never struck me as the kind of man to kill himself, never mind break into a National Trust property to do it.'

Sam threw her an irritated scowl. 'Where do you think he should have gone? The man was an exhibitionist.'

Loveday glanced up, surprised at the unexpected edge to his voice. He had the morning paper in front of him, but she could tell he wasn't really reading it. 'You're very touchy this morning, Sam. Anything wrong?'

'Everything's fine.' He forced a light tone, but he was annoyed with himself for snapping at her. He was already letting the day get on top of him, and it had hardly started. He'd have to do better than this when he came face to face with the man.

Sam tried not to frown, aware that Loveday was still giving him a quizzical look. A confrontation with her now was the last thing he needed, not when he had so much other stuff going on his head. Still, it irritated him that she was even bothered about the self-inflicted demise of an arrogant, unpleasant businessman who had more money than sense.

Loveday carried the two plates to the table and slid one in front of him. Was it her imagination, or was he deliberately avoiding her gaze? She sat down.

'OK Sam,' she said quietly. 'Care to tell me what's going on?'

She'd expected him to bite her nose off again, tell her to stay out of his business, but this dark, lost look in his eyes was something new. Although, now that she thought about it, he'd been distant all week. She'd put it down to an over-heavy workload back at the station in Truro. If that was the case, though, why hadn't he told her? And now there was Silas Venning. If he really had hanged himself in Bolger's Wood, then it wouldn't really involve Sam and his team. And by all accounts, Sam did think it was suicide. Didn't he?

She took another stab at broaching the subject. 'It's Venning, isn't it? You *do* think it's suspicious.'

Sam put down his fork and pushed his chair back from the table with an exasperated sigh. 'I don't want you getting involved in this. I mean it, Loveday. Stay out of it.'

She raised an eyebrow. 'Is that an order, Inspector? You can't tell me what to do.'

Sam opened his mouth to say something, but stopped himself. He really didn't want a row. He put up his hands in a gesture of defeat.

'All I'm saying is: just for once, Loveday, leave this to me.'

Loveday stared at the scrambled egg on her plate. She'd lost her appetite, but she wasn't ready to give up. 'Did you know

Silas had booked a holiday?' She waited. She could tell from Sam's expression that he hadn't, and it gave her a tiny buzz of triumph.

'Laura told me. They were going to Bermuda next month,' she went on, leaning forward. 'Now, why would he do that if he was going to top himself?'

Sam's chair made a scraping noise on the flagged floor as he pushed it further back from the table and stood up.

'You're not going?' Loveday said, glancing at his practically untouched food. 'You haven't had any breakfast.'

'I'm late,' he said briskly, coming round to plant a kiss on top of Loveday's head before striding out of the room.

It was a kiss with little affection. She knew she had annoyed him. Sam didn't like her getting involved in his cases. She never did it on purpose, but she could hardly turn her back when someone asked for her help — not that anyone had in this case, but Venning's death still bothered her. She felt involved because she had so recently been in his home, and had talked with his wife.

On impulse she ran out into the drive after Sam, pulling her robe closer as the sharp sea air stung her face. The rabbits that lived under the hedge surrounding her garden had made an early start, and were already out nibbling the grass beneath her cottage window.

She caught up with him as he was about to get into his old silver-grey Lexus, and tapped him on the shoulder. He turned, looking down at her with a sigh, and gathered her into his arms. 'Sorry,' he whispered into her hair. 'Didn't mean to be so grumpy. It's just a work thing . . . pressure, you know how it is.'

'I'm sorry too,' she said quietly. 'And you're right. I should keep my nose out of your business.'

He gave her a look that said he didn't believe a word of it, and then grinned, kissing the tip of her nose. And before she had a chance to respond, he'd turned again, got into the car, and was off with a backward wave.

Loveday watched his car negotiate the rutted drive until it reached the end and turned right onto the seafront, heading for the A30 and the police headquarters at Truro. For a moment she didn't move, staring out over Mounts Bay. An early mist was rolling in, obscuring the tiny harbour at the foot of St Michael's Mount. The water was still high. She always made a point of monitoring the tides to gauge the best times for her jogs along the beach, so she knew it would soon be receding. In an hour or so the cobbled causeway to the castle would be exposed again, and the milk van could make its delivery to the small general store on the other side.

Loveday shivered and turned back to the cottage. She was about to step inside when the kitchen door at the side of the big house across the way opened and her landlady, Cassie Trevillick, came hurrying out.

'Morning, Cassie,' Loveday called. 'Where's the fire?'

Cassie could be impressively elegant when she bothered. Her tall, model-girl figure and frequently tousled good looks turned many heads. Today she was dressed in a smart grey suit and blue silk blouse. She looked harassed.

'Rush job,' she said. 'And I don't trust that lot down at the marina to actually finish the work on *The Lively Lady* unless I'm there to give their rear ends a kick.'

Loveday walked over to her and managed a grin. 'What way is that to talk about your loyal workforce?'

'Loyal? I should be so lucky. They'd be off in a minute if anyone was daft enough to pay them more than I do.'

Despite her often disorganized personality, Cassie was a talented interior designer who specialized in refurbishing luxury marine craft for rich yacht owners. She had found a niche in the market and was now a successful businesswoman, running her own company. She was also Loveday's best friend.

Cassie nodded back to the house. 'I've had to leave Adam in charge of getting the monsters off to school. He's complaining about being made late for his surgery.'

'You should have asked me,' Loveday said. 'I could have dropped the kids off.'

Cassie waved a hand, dismissing the offer. 'No, he'll manage fine. His patients are used to this.' She yanked open the door of the big 4×4 and then hesitated, turning back. 'Is Sam looking into this terrible business about Silas Venning?'

Loveday pushed back a strand of long, dark hair, and gave her a suspicious smile. 'How did you know about that? Nothing's been announced yet.'

Cassie grinned back. 'Jungle drums . . . you know what this place is like.'

'I didn't realize you knew the Vennings.'

Cassie's nodded. 'Silas has put a few contracts my way.'

'Did he strike you as the kind to take his own life?' The words were out before Loveday could stop herself.

Cassie eyed her keenly. 'Sam doesn't think this is suicide, does he? Was Venning . . . was he murdered?'

'I don't know, Cassie. Sam never discusses his cases with me.' The last thing Loveday wanted was to be responsible for starting rumours, even if she did have her own opinions as to how Silas Venning had met his untimely death.

Cassie was still giving her a doubtful look. 'But you said . . . '

'No, I didn't. I haven't said anything. I only meant . . . ' She paused. 'No, it's nothing. None of my business what Venning's done or hasn't done.'

Cassie gave a sad shrug. 'It's still a shock, though. We just don't know what's going on in other people's lives, do we?' She glanced down at her watch. 'God, is that the time? Sorry, Loveday. I have to go.'

She climbed into the Land Rover and Loveday stepped back as the engine sprung into life. Cassie's hand came out the window in a regal wave as she took off up the drive.

Loveday went back to her warm kitchen with her friend's words ringing in her head. *We just don't know what's going on in other people's lives.* She wondered what was going on in Sam's life right now. Something was troubling him. So why wasn't he sharing it with her? She glanced at the wall clock. He must be near Truro now. She tried to imagine him driving through the early-morning traffic, reaching the city roundabout and cutting off into the police station's staff car park.

* * *

But at the same time as Loveday was picturing the scene, Sam was nowhere near the police station. He had bypassed the city, feeling guiltier by the minute. He'd thought about sharing his intentions with Loveday, of course he had, but would she have understood? Would it even have been fair to burden her with it? This was his problem and he would deal with it, just as he had always promised Tessa that he would.

* * *

Loveday had left her own departure for the magazine office in Truro a bit later than normal, in no mood to cope with the early-morning traffic. She tried to divert her concern for Sam by again going over in her mind her suspicions about Silas Venning's death. The news hadn't yet been made public, but the shocking circumstances surrounding the demise of such a high-profile local man would soon be all round Cornwall. She wondered how Laura was coping. She and Silas had never struck Loveday as a particularly devoted couple, but Silas was her husband. She must have had some feelings for the man.

Loveday recalled the couple's smiling faces in the yachting magazines she'd read. They were high-flyers, sought-after guests at the county's best parties, which was probably why Merrick had suggested doing the article on Laura's artistic skills in the first place.

She remembered gasping in admiration at her first sight of Trevore, the couple's huge white mansion on the banks of the River Fal, when she'd turned up two weeks earlier to interview the woman. The house was magnificent, although the pristinely elegant interior lacked the comfort to make it a welcoming home; but Laura was an artist, Loveday had reminded herself, and maybe artists were like that.

The high ceilings and white walls

throughout the property provided the perfect backdrop for the powerful strokes and swirls of intense colour that were characteristic of the woman's work. It was a house to show off . . . a house to be seen in.

Laura had been waiting to greet Loveday in Trevore's grand front drawing room. The woman rose from one of the two large cream leather sofas that faced each other across a pale green Chinese rug and glass-topped coffee table. Loveday stepped forward, smiling, and took the hand that was offered. A high-mantled white marble fireplace dominated the scene, and a pair of impressive chandeliers glinted in the sunlight that was streaming into the room. Although the two women had spoken on the phone, it was the first time Loveday had met the artist, and she took a moment to assess her. Her first impression was of a handsome woman in her early thirties: tall, with an athletic build, and short, dark hair that was immaculately and expensively styled.

Without preamble Laura said, 'I suppose you will want to see my studio?'

Loveday said she would, and followed the woman back into the big light reception hall with the black-and-white-checked floor.

Laura glided ahead, up the sweeping staircase, past a lovely stained glass window, and stopped by a white-panelled door. She threw it open and said with obvious pride, 'This is where I work.'

Loveday had never seen such a lovely room. Floor-to-ceiling French windows looked out over the river. It was a beautiful morning, and the sun glinted on the water as a pleasure boat, packed with tourists, made its way upstream. At high tide, vessels could sail all the way into Truro; but when the tide was low, passengers would disembark at Malpas and make their way into town by road. Loveday supposed it added an extra dimension to the experience.

'I would find it hard to concentrate with a view like that,' she said, nodding to the window.

Laura's eyes scanned the river, and there was a trace of a contented smile.

'Silas needs to be close to the water.

It's why we chose this house.'

Loveday glanced about her. Paintings in various stages of completion were propped around the room. More canvases were displayed on easels, making Loveday wonder if the room had been staged for her benefit. Laura's emerald silk caftan rustled as she moved from one canvas to the next, describing the ethos behind each work. The paintings were the colours of Cornwall: the aquamarine and deep blues of the sea and sky, the silver-grey granite of the rocks, and the dark, brooding purple of the moors. Loveday was entranced. She wandered around the room studying each one in turn. 'They're wonderful,' she said.

Laura Venning's haughty expression twitched into a smile. 'Yes, they are, aren't they?'

Loveday looked up. The woman obviously wasn't burdened by false modesty. 'Would you mind if I recorded the interview?' she asked, producing her small digital recorder from her bag. 'It's just a back-up for my notes. I delete everything once it's written up.'

'I have no objections. What would you like to ask me?'

Loveday had done her research and already knew some superficial stuff about the woman. She was the only daughter of Geraldine and Graham Anstey, who ran a property empire in Cornwall. Laura was already an established artist when she met and married self-made millionaire Silas Venning. But her paintings still bore her maiden name.

Laura indicated that they should sit. Pen poised, Loveday looked up from her notebook. 'Do either of your parents paint?'

Laura narrowed her dark brown eyes, remembering her childhood. She shrugged. 'No, and neither did I when I was younger. I wanted to be a doctor.' She looked out onto the river, and Loveday wondered again if the view was a distraction when she worked.

'Meredith and I both wanted to study medicine. She carried on, but I lost interest.' She tilted her chin. 'I'd discovered art, you see.' She waved an arm at the windows. 'Who wouldn't want to

15

paint with all of this on your doorstep?'

But Loveday had seen the glint of regret in the woman's eyes, and wondered if medicine had given up on Laura rather than the other way round. 'Meredith?' she asked.

Laura nodded. 'A friend . . . my best friend, actually. She's a doctor now at the hospital in Truro.'

'I see.' Loveday smiled. 'And you don't regret abandoning your first love?'

Laura's elegant eyebrows lifted.

'Medicine, I mean.'

Laura gave her an enigmatic smile, her glance travelling back to the paintings. 'What do you think?'

'I think you are a gifted artist, Mrs Venning.' Loveday paused. 'What does your husband think of your work?'

There was the briefest hesitation before she answered. 'He loves it, of course. And now that it's getting public recognition . . .' She was interrupted by a light knock on the door. It opened, and a small, grey-haired woman, who had earlier answered the door to Loveday, came in carrying a tray of tea things.

'Thank you, Elizabeth,' Laura said, pointing to a small table. 'We'll see to ourselves.' The woman nodded, glancing at Loveday as she put the tray down and hurried out.

'It's Earl Grey, is that all right for you?' Laura was already pouring the tea.

'It's my favourite.' Loveday smiled. She tried to steer the conversation back to Silas as she sipped the hot, fragrant tea, but Laura was clever at fielding questions she didn't want to answer, leaving Loveday curious about her reluctance to talk about her husband.

Film stars, business tycoons and other wealthy people came from all over the world to buy their luxury yachts from the Falmouth-based Venning Marine. At least, that was what she'd been told. As far as Loveday knew, the company was thriving.

The interview was over in less than two hours, and despite her attempts at probing questions, Loveday had the annoying feeling that she hadn't really discovered much more about the woman than she'd already known when she arrived.

'I'll need to see what you are going to

write before it is published, of course,' Laura said, as they moved towards the door.

It wasn't a usual request, but Loveday had no problem with it. 'I'll see to that,' she smiled, shaking Laura's hand as she left.

She had taken quite a few photographs. If her boss, Merrick Tremayne, decided they were good enough, he would go with them. But this was to be a high-profile article, possibly even a front cover for *Cornish Folk*. She'd already decided to suggest commissioning Mylor Ennis, a professional freelance photographer who also did graphic work for the magazine.

But that was then. Any further plans to run the feature had been thrown into turmoil when Sam turned up at Loveday's cottage the previous evening with the news of Silas's apparent suicide. Loveday had rung Merrick for advice, and together they'd decided to leave the final decision about whether or not to run the feature up to Laura herself.

2

'Shocking news about Laura Venning's husband.' Keri Godden looked up from her computer screen as Loveday walked into the office.

Loveday slipped off her jacket and hung it on the ancient coat-stand before sitting down at her desk opposite. She sighed. 'Yes, I'll have to ring her later. I'm not looking forward to it. Merrick wants to give her the chance of pulling out of the publicity if that's what she wants.'

Keri frowned. 'I doubt if that's top of her list of priorities right now. Poor woman. She must be devastated. I mean,' Keri was getting into her stride now, 'I imagine it must be bad enough if your husband dies, but if he deliberately kills himself . . . ' She let the sentence trail off.

Loveday pressed her lips together, staring at her blank computer screen. 'Maybe he didn't,' she said thoughtfully.

Keri looked up quickly. 'OK, Loveday.

Spill. What do you know?' She leaned forward, her eyes eager. 'What has Sam told you?'

Loveday gave her an incredulous stare. Keri was the sweetest of friends, but she'd no idea about the kind of relationship she and Sam had. Why did no one believe Sam didn't discuss his cases with her — well, almost never? 'He's told me absolutely nothing,' she said. 'So I know no more than you, Keri. As far as I can gather, the police are treating Silas Venning's death as suicide.'

'But you don't think it was suicide, do you?' Keri narrowed her eyes. 'Come on, Loveday, you can't fool me.'

Loveday threw up her hands in mock defence. 'I told you. I've no idea.'

Keri gave her one of her half-smiles. 'Really?'

'Yes, really,' she came back, more emphatically than she felt, for she did have some serious reservations about Venning's death being a suicide.

'But it does makes you wonder,' Keri persisted. 'A man like that, going off into the woods to do away with himself.'

That thought was still running through Loveday's mind when the office door swung open and Merrick Tremayne strode in.

'My office, Loveday.' He beckoned to her as he passed her desk. 'I need a word.'

Loveday followed him into the glass-partitioned room that was his office, and waited while he slipped off his tweed jacket and loosened the knot on his yellow tie. He motioned for her to sit.

'So,' he said, pushing his hands through his silvering hair and stretching back in his swivel chair. 'What are we going to do about Laura Venning?'

Loveday shrugged. 'I thought we'd agreed that would be down to her?'

'What does Sam think?' Merrick said. 'Did the man kill himself?'

Loveday put up her hands and shook her head in an exasperated gesture. Another one who assumed she was privy to the collective minds of the Devon and Cornwall Police. 'I honestly have no idea what Sam thinks. I'm usually the last to know.'

Her boss caught the sharpness in her

voice and his head came up. 'Everything all right with you two?'

Loveday said nothing.

'Oh, sorry. None of my business.'

Loveday sighed and shook her head again. 'No, it's not that, Merrick. I know you only have Sam's best interests at heart . . . *our* best interests.' She paused, looking away. *Was* something wrong? Sam could be moody, she was used to that. But this time he was shutting her out — and whatever the problem was, it wasn't just the job, even though that's what he'd told her.

'It's probably nothing,' she said. 'Just me being oversensitive as usual.' She looked across at him. 'You're Sam's best friend, Merrick. Has he said anything to you?'

'About what?'

'About why he's so bloody moody, for a start.'

'We haven't talked about it, no. I expect he just needs some careful handling at the moment.'

She stared at him. 'You *do* know something. You know what's wrong with

Sam.' Her eyes were wary. 'Tell me!'

Merrick swallowed. He'd thought she would have known. Why hadn't Sam talked to her?

'Well? Go on,' Loveday persisted. 'Tell me. I've been going out of my mind here.'

All this cloak and dagger stuff was getting her seriously worried. She held her breath. Sam was ill. That's what Merrick was going to tell her. And if he was ill, then it must be serious. Why else would he have kept it from her?

'It's Tessa,' Merrick said at last. 'Today's Tessa's birthday.'

The words didn't sink in at first. Tessa? And then she knew. 'Oh, God.' She slapped a hand to her forehead and slumped back in her chair. Of course. Why hadn't she remembered? It was true that work was full-on at the moment — there were still five full-page slots to fill, and the current edition of the magazine was due at the printer's before the end of the week. And Sam's workload wasn't exactly light either. But she should have remembered about Tessa.

Her mind scrolled back a year. She and

Sam hadn't been together long, but she'd noticed the change in his mood then too. As the late summer days drew on, he eventually told her.

Tessa, his beautiful, young second wife, had been an artist. She was talented and just beginning to win acclaim for the delicate silver jewellery she made. The little shed at the end of Sam's garden in Stithians had been her workshop. It was still there.

Loveday remembered how the muscles in his jaw had tightened when he told her about the accident — and the drunk driver who took Tessa's life.

So that was it? Loveday blew out her cheeks. 'I should have remembered,' she said quietly.

Merrick sighed. 'Has Sam ever mentioned Brian Penrose to you?'

'Brian Penrose?'

'He was the driver . . . the one responsible for Tessa's accident.'

'No. I don't think he's ever mentioned him by name.'

'Well, the thing is, Loveday . . . '

She almost knew what he was going to

24

say before the words were out.

'Sam has always been adamant that when this man got out of prison he would be there waiting for him.' He paused.

Loveday could feel her heartbeat quicken.

'The thing is . . . it's today. Penrose is due for release from Exeter Prison today.'

Loveday's mouth fell open. That couldn't be right. Sam was in Truro . . . in his office at the police headquarters. Ignoring Merrick's words of caution, she flew out of his office, making straight for her desk. Keri looked up in surprise as Loveday fumbled in her bag for her mobile. When she found it she pressed Sam's number. It went to answerphone. She scrolled through her list of contacts until she found the number for Sam's sergeant, DS Will Tregellis.

'Hi Will. Is Sam with you?' she asked as soon as he answered.

There was a split second's hesitation as Will cleared his throat. 'Er, no. Isn't he with you?'

'Why would he be with me when he's working?' she snapped.

25

Another hesitation, and then, 'He . . . he booked a day's leave.'

Loveday clicked off the call and stared unseeing across the room. Merrick was right. Sam had gone to Exeter Prison. She tried to imagine what he would do when he saw this man. Although he seldom talked about the accident, she knew how much resentment he'd built up about it. He thought two years for killing his beloved Tessa was no punishment at all.

Loveday had tried not to be jealous of the feelings he still had for his late wife. How could she be jealous of a dead woman? But it was there all the same, somewhere at the back of her mind.

Her worry now was what Sam would do. Would he approach the man? Would he strike him? *Would he kill him?* She was trembling.

Keri had come round her desk to put an arm around Loveday's shoulder. 'Loveday, what's happened? Are you ill?'

Merrick appeared, signalling for Keri to pass over Loveday's jacket and bag as he took her arm and led her out of the office.

Loveday was still shaking once they

were sat in a café round the corner, an untouched coffee going cold in front of her.

'You know Sam better than anyone, Merrick. What will he do?' She wished she could stop her teeth from chattering. 'Will Sam kill that man?'

★　★　★

The closer he got to Exeter, the more Sam could feel the familiar anger searing inside him. He tried to rationalize it — tried to focus on Loveday, tried to justify his need for vengeance — but he couldn't. From that moment when he'd met Penrose's arrogant stare from across the courtroom, he'd known what he had to do. In one unforgivable, alcohol-fuelled moment behind the wheel of a stolen car, Brian Penrose had taken the life of the woman Sam had loved. He'd killed Tessa! And for that, Sam could never, *would never*, forgive him.

How many times had he relived the events of that terrible night? Tessa had been excited at meeting up again with her old school chum Verity Langman. It had been years since the two had seen each other, and Sam could still remember how happy she'd been as she left the cottage, turning at the end of the path for a final wave. He didn't worry when she hadn't got home by eleven. The two old friends would have a lot of caching up to do. But when it got to midnight and Tessa still hadn't called him, Sam started to get a sick feeling in the pit of his stomach.

It was Will who had come to his door that night; Sam's old pal, Detective Sergeant Will Tregellis. He'd known instantly, of course, that something terrible had happened. His kids, Jack and Maddie, flashed briefly through his mind, but he'd known it wasn't them. They were safe in Plymouth with their mother, his former wife Victoria. It was Tessa that something had happened to.

Will had been gentle as he told him about the accident . . . about the vehicle that had struck his beloved Tessa as she walked back to her car in the St Ives car park. He hadn't told him the driver didn't stop. Not then.

Even now, Sam remembered the concern on Will's face as they drove to the hospital. They'd taken her to Truro. Tessa's condition was critical. The nurse was grim-faced as she explained that the doctors were doing all they could for her, but it was a serious head injury and it could take some time before there was any definite news.

Not knowing what else to do, Sam had phoned Victoria. He knew she'd come. It seemed right that she should be there. Seeing her, and imagining the children sleeping safely at home, had given Sam a little spike of comfort in the whole terrible nightmare. Victoria had put her arms around him when the young doctor came and told him they couldn't revive Tessa. They had done all they could to save her, he'd said kindly, but she had died.

At first Sam hadn't wanted to leave the hospital, hadn't wanted to leave Tessa alone in this cold, unfamiliar place. But Will had contacted Merrick, and when he arrived, the three of them had somehow managed to coax him away. There was nothing he could do there they'd told him, and so, reluctantly, he allowed himself to be led out of the hospital.

He was never quite sure what had happened next, but they must have taken him to Merrick's house — an old converted farmhouse on the outskirts of Truro — because he woke up next morning in an unfamiliar room. When he'd dragged himself out of bed and gone to the window, it was morning, and Merrick's housekeeper, Connie Bishop, was standing by the door with a cup of tea in her hand. She bit her lip and Sam thought he saw a trace of tears as she bustled past him and put the mug down beside the bed.

She turned, giving Sam a solemn look. 'We are all so very sorry, sir . . . ' But her voice dried up and she couldn't finish the sentence.

Sam had nodded and turned away, the lump in his throat choking him. He couldn't allow the woman to see that. He really couldn't cope with her sympathy.

Connie cleared her own throat. 'Mr Tremayne says to come down whenever you're ready.'

Ready? Sam had thought. *Ready for what?* He would never be ready to accept that he'd lost his lovely Tessa. But he'd nodded and said, 'Thanks, Connie. Tell Merrick I'll be down shortly.'

He found them in the kitchen. Merrick had got to his feet as Sam walked in. The look of sorrow in his friend's eyes had been unbearable. How would he get through this if his friends pitied him? He had only one question. 'Did they catch him?' He barked out the words in a hoarse voice.

Merrick had nodded. 'He's in custody.'

Sam turned on his heel, his eyes glinting cold steel. But Merrick was right beside him. 'Where are you going, Sam? I said the man is in custody. Let your colleagues deal with this.'

Sam's shoulders were rigid. 'I need to see him, Merrick.' The muscles in his jaw tightened. 'I need to see the scum that killed Tessa.'

'And you will,' Merrick said gently, turning Sam back into the kitchen. 'But maybe just not today.'

★　★　★

Sam's hands tightened on the steering wheel, and he forced himself to relax his grip as his thoughts returned to the present. He was on the A30, less than forty minutes from the prison. He had no idea what time Penrose would be released, but he'd guessed it would be early, certainly before visitors were due to arrive. Sam muttered a curse. He should have checked the visiting hours, but he doubted if they would start much before 2pm. He glanced at the clock on the dashboard. It was almost ten. He could have a long wait. He wondered what Penrose would be doing now. He tried to imagine him in his cell. Would he be excited? Would there be a big gathering of family and friends waiting to greet him when he stepped from behind that prison door?

The traffic had lessened as he approached the city, and he could feel his heartbeat accelerate. A few more minutes and he would be there. A white Clio was turning off at the junction just ahead of him. For a second he thought it was Loveday — or was that his guilty conscience taking over? She had no idea he had been planning this. He hadn't mentioned Penrose's release date to her, although he'd known it for weeks. Merrick knew, of course. There was nothing he could hide from his old friend. He could read Sam like a book. But he felt guilty about not telling Loveday. He tried to justify that by convincing himself that he was just sparing her any hurt. But, deep down, he knew the real reason was that Loveday would try to stop him doing what he was now. He found a parking place in the car park near the prison and walked to the main door.

Exeter Prison was an old, red-brick, Victorian establishment that had originally been built for just over three hundred inmates. Sam knew it now housed more than five hundred offenders. On this dull, grey morning it looked austere. He moved to a corner where he could shelter from the wind, and pulled up the collar of his coat.

Sam had read stories about this place from when it had been a setting for executions, more than a hundred years earlier.

He vaguely recalled the details of a

bizarre case when three attempts to execute a prisoner had all ended in failure. Apparently a trapdoor in the scaffold had failed to open. Sam shivered, narrowing his eyes into the wind. The story had had a happy ending: the prisoner's sentence was later commuted to life imprisonment, and after several petitions to the then Home Secretary, he was released — even if he'd had to wait some twenty years for his freedom.

The blue wooden door at the front of Exeter Prison didn't open until 11.30. Sam steeled himself, waiting for the man to emerge.

Brian Penrose was smaller than he'd remembered; thinner, too. He stood by the road, frail and vulnerable-looking, not glancing back at the building in which he had been incarcerated for the past two years. There was no sign of anyone coming to meet him. Sam could feel his heart pumping. He had visualized this moment so many times.

Penrose had done his time, but two years was nothing for taking Tessa's life. This was Sam's moment to get even. A life for a life. That would be the only fair outcome. He was going to beat the man to a pulp with his bare hands.

He tried to start forward, but his feet wouldn't move. The man looked so pathetic. Whatever had happened to him inside hadn't been good. But Sam hadn't driven all this way to let him just walk away. He clenched his fist, feeling the life coming back to his feet. In a handful of strides he could be across that road, his fist at Penrose's throat. He began to move forward.

The car came from nowhere, tyres screeching as it shot past him. Sam saw the look of shock in Penrose's eyes turn to terror as he realized what was about to happen. There was a scream, and then a sickening thud as the car slammed into Penrose, catapulting his body into the air. It hit the ground with a thump as the driver gunned up his engine and roared off at speed.

For a split second everything froze. Even from where he stood across the road, Sam could tell that Penrose was dead.

★ ★ ★

'Your coffee's gone cold, Loveday. Shall I get you another?' Merrick said, rising from the table.

Loveday was about to refuse when her mobile rang. Her eyes widened when she recognized the caller. 'It's Laura Venning,' she said, staring at the phone.

Merrick sat back down again and gave a little wave, telling her to answer it. This was all they needed. It had been less than twenty-four hours since Silas Venning's body had been discovered. Laura would want to stop the article. Loveday cleared her throat. 'Laura!' She swallowed. 'I was so sorry to hear about Silas.'

'Oh, you know?' Laura Venning said, giving a hopeless little sigh. 'Yes, of course you would.' She hesitated, choosing her words. 'I need to see you, Loveday. Can you come over?'

'Well, yes, of course . . . ' She felt a sudden rush of compassion for the woman. 'You're not on our own, are you?'

'As a matter of fact, I am.' Laura's voice was brittle. No show of emotion.

Loveday was already reaching for her jacket.

'I'm leaving now,' she said, but the phone connection had already been cut. Loveday began to struggle into her jacket.

'Hang on,' Merrick said, getting up to block her exit. 'You can't just go rushing off like this. I thought we were talking.'

'What's the point? Sam's switched his phone off. There's nothing either of us can do to help him if he doesn't want to be helped.' She glanced at her watch. It was already 11.45. 'And by now, whatever was going to happen, probably *has* happened.'

Half an hour earlier Loveday had been sick with worry for Sam, but now she was just plain angry. He hadn't trusted her enough to confide in her. Whether his late wife was dead or alive, it was still Tessa that he loved. And if he'd been prepared to kill for her . . . A wave of nausea swept over Loveday. She had to stop herself thinking like this.

There were no other cars in the drive as she pulled up at the side of the big white house. All the way there, she had forced every thought of Sam from her mind. But no doubt he'd be accusing her of interfering again when he heard about this visit. That is, if he wasn't in jail himself by then.

Loveday took another glance around. It was odd that the place seemed so deserted. By all accounts, Laura and Silas had a huge circle of friends. So where were they?

Loveday had expected a wan-faced Laura to open the door, eyes red-rimmed from crying, but there were no signs of a sleepless night on this face; no outward evidence of any grief at all, in fact. Perhaps this was how the woman dealt with trauma. The tears would come later. Her first instinct was to reach out, offer comfort and soothing words, but Loveday sensed Laura Venning would not welcome such gestures. She followed her through the airy hall and into the drawing room. The enormous windows had the same view as the ones in the studio upstairs, but today angry dark clouds loomed, and the river mirrored the sky's gloomy mood.

'Thank you for coming, Loveday.' Laura's

voice was brisk as she waved Loveday to sit on one of the two huge sofas.

Loveday touched her arm. 'You shouldn't be on your own, not today. Can I call someone for you . . . one of your friends, perhaps?'

'My parents are on their way home from the Caribbean. They'll be here by tonight.' Laura's controlled behaviour was wrong-footing Loveday. She wasn't sure how to react. She cleared her throat.

'It must have been such a shock for your parents, too.'

Laura frowned, ignoring the question. She said, 'It hasn't been on the news. Why would that be?' She rounded on Loveday. 'You're a journalist. You must know.'

Was this was why she'd been invited — to be pumped for information? Loveday shrugged. 'I'm not a newspaper journalist any more. The police don't usually release this kind of information to magazines.'

'But you must have contacts in the police?' She'd been pacing the room and suddenly swung round to meet Loveday's confused stare, and then her expression softened. 'I'm sorry. I don't know what you must think of me.' She sank onto the sofa. 'They won't tell me anything, you see; only that Silas was found hanging from a . . . ' Her voice trailed into silence, and for the first time Loveday thought she saw a sparkle of tears in the dark eyes.

'The police probably don't know any more than that,' she said gently.

Laura looked up, eyes defiant again. 'Silas didn't kill himself!'

Loveday swallowed, trying to find the right words. 'I can't imagine what you must be going through . . . '

'We were going to Bermuda next month. I told you that the last time you were here, didn't I?'

Loveday nodded.

'And he'd booked an appointment with his dentist on Friday,' Laura went on, agitation now in her voice. 'Now, why would he do that if he was going to kill himself?' She paused, glancing out over the river. 'And besides, he had no reason to. He was happy. We were happy.'

'Your husband had no business worries?' Loveday probed gently.

Laura shook her head. 'Of course not.

Venning Marine is thriving. Ask anyone.'
She got up and went to a table of drinks
behind the sofa. She lifted a bottle of
vodka and waggled it at Loveday. 'Will
you join me?'

Loveday shook her head. Laura was
returning to her seat, glass in hand, when
the doorbell rang. She put her drink on
the long glass coffee table and looked up,
frowning. 'Can you see to that? Tell them
I'm resting or something. I don't want to
see anyone today.'

Loveday's eyebrow lifted. She wasn't
sure she appreciated being ordered about
like one of this woman's lackeys, but
under the circumstances . . . She stood
up and went to the door.

Meredith Deering didn't wait to be
invited in. She swept past Loveday into
the drawing room, and threw her arms
around Laura.

'I'm sorry,' Loveday said helplessly. 'I
tried to stop her.'

'It's fine, Loveday. I didn't mean to
keep Meredith out.' She turned and went
to pour the newcomer a drink. Loveday
sank back onto the sofa. Something was

going on here, something she hadn't yet worked out. If Laura believed her husband hadn't killed himself, the implication was that someone else had — and that was murder! So why wasn't she telling all this to the police?

'Have they told you how it happened?' Meredith asked, her green eyes moist.

Laura shook her head. 'Not a word. How did you hear?'

'Radio Cornwall. It was on the eleven o'clock bulletin.' Meredith looked away, biting her lip. 'It said the police were treating it as an unexplained death.'

Laura's eyes widened. 'That means suicide, doesn't it?'

'No, Laura,' Loveday said, quickly. 'It just means that the police don't yet know how Silas died.'

But the woman wasn't listening. She jumped up and began pacing the room again. 'I knew there was something that Detective Inspector Kitto wasn't telling me.' Loveday stiffened at the mention of Sam's name. She tried to cover it, but Laura had been watching her. 'You know him?'

Loveday looked away. She was in no

mood to be questioned about Sam. 'We've met,' she said, trying for a noncommittal tone.

Meredith hadn't touched her drink. 'I can't believe you're taking this so calmly. Are you sure you're all right, Laura? Maybe I should give you something to help you sleep.'

But Laura swept the offer aside, holding her friend's concerned stare. 'When did you last see Silas, Meredith?'

Was it Loveday's imagination, or had the faintest tinge of colour just touched the newcomer's cheeks?

Meredith tucked a stray lock of blonde hair behind her ear and forced a smile. 'It would have been the yacht club dinner two weeks ago, wouldn't it?'

'Not since then?' Laura persisted.

Meredith shook her head. 'No, why do you ask?'

'Because he didn't kill himself, and I want everyone who knew him to back me up. If Silas had been planning something like this, I would have known.' Laura shook her head. 'I would just have known.'

Loveday leaned forward. 'You noticed

43

nothing unusual about your husband's behaviour in the last few days?'

'I just said so, didn't I?' Laura snapped, then immediately put out a hand. 'I'm sorry. It's just that . . .'

Meredith's head jerked up and she stared at her friend, as though she had just realized the implication of what was being suggested. 'You can't really believe someone . . .' Her voice shook. 'That someone murdered Silas?'

Laura's shoulders lifted in a shrug. 'What other explanation could there be?'

Meredith had gone deathly pale, and Loveday saw her hand shake as she reached for her glass.

'And this is what you want to tell the police?' She looked askance.

'Unless you can suggest any reason why Silas might kill himself, Meredith?'

Meredith moistened her lips. It was a few moments before she spoke. 'Maybe I can.' She hesitated. 'Silas came to see me at the hospital last week . . . as a friend.'

'But you just said the last time you saw him was at the yacht club dinner two weeks ago . . .'

44

'I know what I said. I . . . I lied.'

Laura was staring at her, eyes narrowed.

'Silas had a serious heart problem,' Meredith said. 'It was treatable, but he didn't want you to know about it, not yet. I told him before that he had to take things easier, but he just needed more reassurance. That's what the trip to the Bahamas was about.' She swallowed. 'I suggested it ages ago.'

Laura strode across the room to the window and stood with her back to them. 'I want you to leave now, Meredith,' she said.

'Please, Laura,' her friend pleaded. 'It wasn't up to me to tell you.'

'And close the door on your way out.'

Loveday heard Meredith gasp, before she turned on her heel and marched out of the room. Laura didn't turn back until they both heard the door slam. 'I think you should go too.' She gave a little sigh. 'Look, I appreciate you coming over, but I need to be on my own right now.'

'Of course,' Loveday said, getting to her feet. She wasn't happy about leaving

Laura alone in her present mood, but she couldn't force the woman to let her stay.

Laura suddenly swung round to look Loveday in the eye.

'And about that article . . . I want you to publish it.'

'Really? Are you sure that's what you want?'

Laura nodded.

Loveday turned to go, and then hesitated, looking back. 'Will you be all right on your own here?'

Laura was replenishing her glass.

'Are you sure I can't call someone for you?' She met the woman's dark stare.

'You can call the police. I don't know what game Meredith is playing, but Silas didn't kill himself. If he was ill he would have treated it as a challenge, not been defeated by it.' She came forward and touched Loveday's arm. 'Meredith knows something. The police need to talk to her.'

3

Loveday sat for a moment in her car before starting the engine. This was turning into a very disturbing day. Laura Venning's mention of the police had sent her mind into another whirl about what Sam was up to in Exeter. She had long since dismissed the thought that he would have gone there to kill Brian Penrose. Sam didn't kill people. He might not be averse to punching the man in the face, though — and that was assault. Loveday tried not to think about the consequences of that.

And now here was Laura Venning suggesting her husband had been murdered.

Loveday followed the twisting lane back up to the main road. It was almost one o'clock. She turned on the car radio to catch the lunchtime news. Would the bulletin about Silas Venning have changed? She listened.

'*Tributes are coming in for the Cornish*

businessman, *Silas Venning, whose body was found in Bolger's Woods yesterday. A spokesman for Cornwall Police said they were not yet in a position to confirm a cause of death. Investigations are continuing.'*

Loveday was about to switch off the radio when the announcer continued, *'News is just coming in about a fatal accident outside Exeter Prison. A man has died after being struck by a car outside the main door. It is understood that the driver of the vehicle failed to stop.*

'Police are appealing for witnesses to the incident; in particular, for anyone who saw a light-coloured car drive away from the scene at high speed.'

Loveday's heart stopped. Sam! This couldn't have anything to do with Sam — could it? She could feel the panic rising inside her. She pulled into the side of the road, her hands shaking as she rummaged in her bag for her phone. She rang Sam's number. Still no answer. His phone was still switched off! She tried Merrick. He was engaged. *Oh God, Sam!* Her breath was coming in short bursts

48

now. *What have you done?*

Loveday had no recollection of how she got back to Truro, or of driving into the magazine's staff car park. She was taking the back stairs up to the editorial floor two at a time. Heads lifted as she burst into the office, but she ignored them, making straight for Merrick's room.

'Have you heard the news? It's Sam, isn't it?' she gasped. 'He's killed Brian Penrose!'

Merrick crossed the room and pulled out a chair for her, his hand making an 'everything's fine' gesture to the worried faces on the other side of the glass wall. 'Sit down, Loveday, and stop being so melodramatic,' he said, but he was smiling. 'Sam had nothing to do with what happened in Exeter. He . . . '

But his words were cut short by the ringing of Loveday's phone. She dived into her bag, her heart hammering when she saw Sam's name flash up on the tiny screen.

She sank onto the chair. 'Sam! Are you all right?'

'I'm fine, Loveday. And I'm so sorry.

You must have been worried.'

'Worried!' she exploded. 'You think I must have been *worried*?' She was desperately trying to control her anger. 'I've been going out of my mind here.' She paused. 'I take it you're in Exeter?'

For a second there was silence, and then in a sheepish voice, Sam said, 'Yes, I'm in Exeter. I should have told you, I'm sorry . . .'

'And Penrose?' she cut in sharply.

'He's dead . . . and it happened right there in front of me.'

'But you didn't . . . I mean, it wasn't you driving that car, was it?'

'What?' Sam's voice blasted down the phone. 'Well, of course it wasn't me driving the car. You didn't think I was going to kill him, did you?'

'I . . . er . . .' Loveday started, but he wasn't listening.

'I went there to see Penrose . . . to leave him in no doubt that I would be watching him from now on. There was no way he was getting away with thinking it was all over. He owed Tessa more than that.'

'But you didn't kill him . . .' Loveday

whispered, her voice weak with relief. She would get angry with him again later for keeping her in the dark. Right now, all she wanted to do was to wrap her arms around him.

'Look, I know I should have told you I was going to see Penrose today.' His voice was gentle now. 'I just didn't want to involve you in any of this. Penrose was my problem. I didn't want to upset you, Loveday.'

She fought back a bubble of hysterical laughter. *He didn't want to upset her? Really?*

'I've had to hang around and give the police up here a statement, but I'm on my way back now. Don't bother cooking tonight, Loveday. I'll pick up a bottle of wine and a takeaway.'

And with that he was gone.

'Well?' Merrick urged. 'What did Sam say?'

Loveday beamed tearfully at him. 'He said he's picking up a takeaway.'

Merrick shook his head, laughing. 'So he's not in jail, then?'

'Not yet, but he is in big trouble when

he gets back.' She squirmed in her chair on the opposite side of Merrick's desk. 'Sam really doesn't have a clue how much anguish he caused me today.'

'I don't imagine he does. He would never have gone off like that if he'd thought the thing out.' Merrick smiled. 'Don't be too hard on him, Loveday. It could have been a lot worse.'

'I know,' she said quietly. 'But he's still in big trouble with me when he gets home.'

Merrick linked his fingers behind his head and his chair creaked alarmingly as he leaned back.

'Tell me what happened with Laura Venning. I'm assuming we'll be dropping the feature?'

'Oh, no.' Loveday grimaced. 'Sorry, Merrick. I should have rung you straight away, but with all this . . . ' She threw her hands in the air. 'No, she's definitely happy for the piece to go ahead. She just wants some additional stuff putting in about her husband. I think she's seeing it as a tribute to her bravery in the face of grief . . . something like that.'

Merrick arched an eyebrow. 'And you've agreed to this?'

Loveday shrugged. 'Why not? I actually kind of like the idea.'

'Well, if that's what she wants . . . '

'It's why she wants it that worries me,' Loveday said. 'Laura Venning is quite a strange woman. She's convinced her husband was murdered, you know.'

Merrick pursed his lips. 'Is she, now? I wonder what Sam will have to say about that?'

Loveday tut-tutted. 'You know better than that, Merrick. I'm the last person he would confide in. He'd do anything to stop me from getting involved.'

Merrick chuckled. 'Sam knows you so well, Loveday. But he's right, of course: you should leave it to him. He worries about you, and not without good reason.'

'Sam doesn't have the monopoly on worrying about people you care for,' she said.

'No, but you've had enough narrow escapes to be going on with. Let the police find out what happened to Silas Venning.'

'Did I say otherwise?'

'I'm warning you, Loveday,' he called after her as she left his office. 'Stay out of this one.'

Her hand hovered over the phone as she sat at her desk. Keri's seat opposite was empty. Should she call Sam back and tell him what Laura had said? She pressed her lips together, staring at her computer screen, and then began tapping the keys.

She was scanning through some background pictures of Silas Venning when Keri swept back into the room and tapped her shoulder. 'Feeling better now?' she asked.

Loveday nodded. 'Much better, thanks.'

'Care to share what the problem was?'

'Later,' Loveday said, glancing up at the younger girl. 'I promise.'

Keri was looking over her shoulder. 'Why are you Googling Silas Venning?'

'I'm not sure . . . just a feeling.'

'Quite the party animals,' Keri said, watching the scroll of images showing Silas and Laura at various high profile county events. Then she peered closer. 'Isn't that your friend, Cassie Trevillick?'

Loveday squinted at the screen. It definitely was Cassie. She hadn't mentioned being a guest at one of the Vennings' parties — and where was Adam? But Keri had moved on. She pointed to the glamorous blonde that Silas appeared to have draped himself over.

'Who's that?'

Meredith Deering was wearing a navy-and-white sailing top, and the skimpiest white shorts Loveday had ever seen. They were on the Vennings' yacht, *The Lively Lady*. Laura was in the background, waving a champagne glass about.

'She's a doctor at the hospital here in Truro.'

Keri narrowed her eyes. 'Hmm . . . is she really?'

Loveday glanced back at the picture and checked the date. She frowned. 'This was published only a couple of weeks ago.'

'So?'

'Well, Dr Deering told Laura that Silas had a heart condition. She even suggested it might be the reason he took his own life.' She tilted her head at the screen. 'Does he look like a man with a heart condition?'

Keri's eyebrow arched. 'Not the operable kind. From the way he's looking at that sexy doctor, I'd say it was a completely different kind of heart condition.'

'Exactly what I was thinking. So why would she say that if it wasn't true? She of all people would know a post-mortem would show up any kind of problem.'

Keri shrugged. 'Beats me. You're the detective.'

Loveday threw her a scowl as she hit the print button. The image of Meredith and Silas looking so cosy, while Laura looked on in the background, stayed with her for the rest of the day.

★ ★ ★

It was dark when Loveday got back to her cottage in Marazion, and Sam's car was already in the drive. She'd been going over in her head what to say to him, but she was distracted by the weird sensation of her feelings being somewhere between sheer relief and fizzing anger. Sam still had much explaining to do. Surely he must have known how worried she would be when he just took off for Exeter without a word of explanation? Loveday stared at the cottage, trying to feel comforted by the knowledge that Sam was inside waiting for her, but she was frowning. It wasn't easy, living with the knowledge that your man was still in love with his dead wife.

Sam had heard the car, and the door of the cottage opened before Loveday had even switched off the engine. He held out his arms, and Loveday ran into them. The pleasure of seeing him again sent all her doubts melting away, like rain on the first delicate snows of winter.

'Sam . . . oh, Sam.' The relief of seeing him here — and safe — was overwhelming. Tears were spilling down her cheeks.

He wiped them away with gentle fingers. 'I'd have been home sooner if I'd known I'd get this kind of welcome.'

'Oh, for heaven's sake,' Loveday said,

embarrassed by the unbidden show of emotion. She swiped crossly at her wet cheeks and pulled away from him. 'And just where do you think you've been?'

Sam put his hands up as though in defence. But he was still grinning at her.

'Let's talk about this inside,' he said.

The delicious aroma of Chinese food filled the kitchen. He'd been as good as his word. There was a takeaway keeping warm in the oven. But right at that moment, a large glass of wine was what she needed most.

He read her thoughts and told her to go through to the fire he'd lit while he fetched some glasses. The September evening was chilly, and it was good to see a blaze crackling in the hearth. Loveday sank into her favourite chair and stretched luxuriously.

'So,' she said, when Sam had returned with full glasses and settled himself on the sofa. 'You went to Exeter today. Care to expound on that?'

'Only if you're prepared to listen,' he said, trying to keep his voice light.

'I'm all ears,' Loveday said.

Sam took a long sip of his wine. 'I should have explained all this properly to you before now. There was no reason why you should have known that today is Tessa's birthday.'

Loveday felt a tiny spike of ice jab at her heart. Of course she should have known. She should have remembered.

'It was also the day Brian Penrose was due for release.' He looked up at her and his eyes darkened. 'Penrose was the drunk driver . . . '

'I know,' Loveday said quickly. 'Merrick told me.'

Sam stared into the flames. 'Less than three years for taking another person's life, and always destined to be out in two. Tessa deserved better. I drove up to Exeter today to thump the living daylights out of him.'

'I'm very glad you didn't,' Loveday interrupted. 'That kind of thing wouldn't look good on your otherwise unblemished police record.'

'I know, but the red mist had come down, and I wasn't exactly thinking straight. I'd visualized that moment so many times. I imagined seeing him come sauntering out of the prison door — and me waiting for him.'

He lifted his glass and took another slug of wine. 'It was surreal. I was standing on the other side of the road, waiting for that big blue door to open. Eventually, it did, and this scrawny, nervous-looking bloke just kind of crept out.

'At the trial, Penrose just looked like an arrogant young kid. There was no sign of remorse for what he'd done. Oh, he told the court he was sorry, said he was just a few beers over the limit. It wasn't really his fault.' Sam took another gulp of wine and looked across at her. 'Are you surprised I wanted to beat the life out of him?'

Loveday sprang forward to take his glass from him and put her arms round him. 'I'm so sorry, Sam.' For the first time, she was able to put herself in his shoes. He had lost the woman he loved, and the cocky young tyke responsible for that thought he'd done nothing wrong. It was no wonder Sam had harboured thoughts of revenge all these years.

'What happened next?' she asked quietly.

Sam took a deep breath. 'I got a shock when I saw him. I'd been expecting him to emerge full of swagger — as he'd appeared the last time I saw him — but that had all gone. He looked so pathetic standing there, not knowing what to do. I don't know what happened to him in prison, but something must have because Penrose was a changed man.

'I'd spent so long imagining the satisfaction I'd get from punching this individual, and then suddenly there seemed no point. Just seeing Penrose in that condition . . . well, I actually felt sorry for him. But I still couldn't let him off the hook. He needed to know I'd be on his case. I'd started towards him when there was this God-awful screeching of tyres.' Sam's eyes narrowed into slits as he remembered. 'The car came out of nowhere. I could see what was about to happen and tried to lunge forward, but I couldn't even do that. I just kind of froze. I don't really know what I thought I could do. Nobody could have saved Penrose.'

He shook his head with a sigh. 'I can still hear the sickening sound as the vehicle slammed into him. Penrose cartwheeled into the air and landed in the road with a terrible thud. The car just roared off.'

Loveday's eyes widened in horror. 'Did you see the driver?'

Sam shook his head. 'Not really. His collar was pulled up, covering half his face, and he had one of those woolly hats pulled down over his brow.'

'What about the car then? Any reg number?'

'Yes, I got that, and I've passed it on to the local plods, but I've no doubt it had been stolen. It's probably a burned-out shell by now.'

'Wow,' Loveday said. 'You certainly see life, Detective Inspector Kitto.'

'You could say that,' Sam said. 'Or you could just say that there were more than just me with a score to settle with Mr Penrose today.'

'You think his killing is related to something that happened in prison?'

'I don't know,' Sam said, 'but I intend to find out.'

Loveday frowned. 'Isn't that down to Exeter Police now? It happened well out of your patch, Sam.'

'Penrose came from Redruth,' Sam said. 'I'll be starting there.'

4

Loveday was wakened early next morning by the drumming of the water in the shower. It was still dark outside when she wandered into the kitchen to fill the kettle. Glancing to the window, she could see lights in Cassie and Adam's house across the yard, and smiled. She could imagine the lively Sophie and Leo bounding into their parents' bedroom and demanding their breakfast. It all seemed so normal compared to what was going on in her own life.

Sam was shaved and dressed when he appeared ten minutes later, and Loveday was relieved to see he looked none the worse after yesterday's traumatic events. In fact, he looked invigorated. She should be happy. After all, he hadn't killed anyone. And in Loveday's mind yesterday, that had been a strong possibility. She pushed her fingers through her hair and asked him what he would like for breakfast.

'I'll do it,' Sam said, indicating she should sit.

She watched as he put bread in the toaster and poured boiling water onto the instant coffee grounds in their mugs.

She still hadn't mentioned her previous day's visit to the Vennings' place. Last night's revelations of events outside Exeter Prison had been dramatic enough. But the Vennings were still important. Should she tell him Laura was convinced her husband had been murdered? He'd say it was none of her business. And anyway, if the PM report on Venning indicated anything suspicious, then it would be investigated. He was right; it was police work, and nothing to do with her.

'OK, what's up?' Sam's voice interrupted her thoughts. She'd been miles away, wrestling with her conscience about how much to share of the visit to Laura Venning.

She pulled her mind back to the present. 'Nothing's up. I'm still half-asleep, that's all.'

The toast popped up and she rose to

attend to it, but Sam turned her back and caught her hands. She looked up at him and saw the concern in his eyes.

'I'm fine, Sam, honestly.' She released herself from his grip and sat back down at the table.

'You're still worried about what happened yesterday. I've apologized for going off like that and not telling you. I've explained it. I thought you understood.'

She had understood, but this was another day; and now, instead of seeking his revenge on Brian Penrose, Sam was going off to find his killer. It was all still about Tessa.

★ ★ ★

It was only just beginning to get light as Sam's Lexus left the dark ripples of Mounts Bay behind and took the roundabout to the A30, bound for Truro.

He was worried about Loveday. There had been none of her usual sparkle this morning. And she was hiding something. He could tell. Was it his fault? He hadn't trusted her enough to tell her what he was planning yesterday. She would have tried to stop him for sure, she might even have insisted on going with him, but that wouldn't have been right. Penrose was a demon he had to lay down by himself — but now someone had done it for him. He sighed. It had never been his wish that Penrose should die, just that he should be made to show a little remorse for the terrible thing he did. None of that mattered now. It was out of his hands. A young thug in a stolen car had seen to that.

Yesterday he'd still been suffering from shock on that drive back to Cornwall, but there had been a new feeling too — a kind of release. There was nothing more he could do for Tessa; he knew that now. He would never forget her, but it was time to let go of the past. He had a new life now with Loveday; at least, he hoped he had. He'd almost blown that by chasing off to Exeter yesterday. He should have told her what he'd been planning — or, better still, not gone there at all.

He pulled out to pass a slow-moving delivery lorry in front of him at the same time as its driver had a similar idea. Sam braked and allowed the vehicle out. The driver ahead hadn't checked his mirror. Sam muttered a curse; the road was busy, and the idiot could have caused a serious accident. He doubted if the man even knew what had almost happened. He kept his frustration in check as he neared the main roundabout into the city. His mind was reeling through yesterday's terrible image of Penrose being mowed down by the hit-and-run driver. He couldn't bring the man back to life, but there was one thing he could do for him. He could find his killer!

* * *

Loveday was getting into her car when Cassie appeared at her kitchen door and called out to her, 'I don't suppose you're free for lunch today?'

Loveday's mind scrolled through the appointments she could remember. She had arranged to interview a couple who had opened a hotel for pets in St Ives, and she was already running late. There was a mountain of writing and editing to do back at the office — and then this situation with Laura Venning. She knew she couldn't ignore that, no matter what Sam told her.

'Sorry, Cassie. I really don't — '

'Coffee, then? Surely you could find time for a coffee?' Cassie bit her lip. 'I really need to speak to you, Loveday.'

'Well . . . of course, if it's that important.' Loveday searched her friend's face. 'Everything is all right, isn't it, Cassie?' She nodded back towards the house. Cassie and Adam were one the happiest couples she knew, and their children were adorable. They were like family to Loveday.

'No, no, nothing like that,' Cassie said. 'But I do need your advice, and sooner rather than later would be good.'

Loveday gave her a suspicious grin. 'Are you being deliberately mysterious to get me hooked?'

Cassie put on her innocent expression.

'OK,' Loveday laughed. 'But it will have to be the café next to the office. I won't have time to go elsewhere.'

'Thanks, Loveday. I appreciate this,'

Cassie said, before turning to hurry back to the house.

Loveday sighed as she drove down the back road to St Ives, wondering what could be troubling her friend. It was one more thing for her to worry about.

* * *

'Are you sure you should be doing this, boss?' DS Will Tregellis was studying Sam with an anxious frown.

'Perfectly sure,' Sam said.

'You don't think maybe you are still a bit close to the whole thing?'

'That's exactly why it should be me who visits Penrose's parents,' Sam said, throwing down the pen he had been fiddling with. 'I was there when the man was killed, Will. It happened right in front of me and I did nothing.'

'But it was a hit-and-run. What could you possibly have done to prevent it?'

Sam sighed. 'I don't know, but I feel I should have done something.'

Will had never asked what Sam had been doing outside the prison. He didn't have to; Sam was well aware of the sympathy his colleagues felt over his loss. They had all been so supportive when Tessa was killed. They also knew his fury at the injustice of her killer's short sentence. And now he was about to face the man's parents. Would they hold him responsible for their son's death? He could only hope not.

Eileen and Eric Penrose lived in a small red-brick terraced house in the centre of Redruth. It was much like the place where Sam had grown up himself. Although his parents were no longer alive, the house was still standing. He'd caught a glimpse of it as he and Will drove through the town. There was a baby buggy in the front garden. The sight was strangely comforting. It made him think of his children Jack and Maddie in Plymouth. He didn't see nearly enough of them.

He was aware that Will was watching him as they negotiated the broken paving slabs to the Penrose's front door. It was opened almost as soon as Sam had pressed the bell. The elderly man who stood there peered out at them with a frown. Both detectives produced their ID cards. The man shrugged and shuffled backwards, allowing them into the dark airless hall. 'The wife's through there,' he said. 'You'd better go through.'

A stout woman, who Sam judged to be in her sixties, sat in a chair by the fire.

'Mrs Penrose?' Sam enquired.

The woman nodded. Her husband had come in behind them, and took the chair opposite his wife. The detectives had not been invited to sit.

'I am Detective Inspector Kitto, and this is Detective Sergeant Tregellis,' Sam said, looking from one to the other. 'Can I ask your names?'

The man gave them a sullen stare. 'I'm Eric. She's Eileen.'

'We are very sorry for your loss,' Sam said, addressing his remarks to the woman. 'We understand what a difficult time this must be for you both, but if we are to find the person driving the car that killed your — '

'Kitto?' Eileen Penrose was staring at Sam with shining beady eyes that missed nothing. 'You said your name was Kitto?'

Sam nodded.

'It was your wife in that accident, wasn't it?'

Sam heard Will catch his breath. He fought the urge to fire out — *'That's right, it was my wife that your son killed.'* But instead, he took a breath himself, and nodded again.

The woman leaned forward in her chair. 'I'm very sorry, Mr Kitto. It should never have happened. Our Brian was vexed about that. He deserved to go to inside, he knew that.' Her voice broke, and she reached into her apron pocket and drew out a crumpled hankie. 'He didn't deserve what happened to him, though. Not that.' She shook her head and dabbed the hankie to her eyes. 'He was moving back in here. It was all planned. There was a job waiting for him and everything.'

Sam cleared his throat. 'We think your son was deliberately killed, Mrs Penrose. Can you think of anyone who would want to harm him?'

Eileen Penrose gave him a sharp

glance, and he thought she was thinking, *Apart from you, you mean?*

She switched her attention to her husband, who was staring vacantly into the fire. 'Plenty of them thugs had it in for Brian; that's right, isn't it, Eric?'

Eric shrugged. 'The boy's gone, love. What does it matter now?'

'What are you saying? Of course it matters,' she snapped. 'Our Brian was scared in that place. He knew they were after him.'

Sam stared at her. 'Who was after him?'

'The ones in jail with him. They threatened him. He was terrified. That's why he was so happy he was getting out; he could get away from them, see.'

'Do you know the names of any of these people who threatened Brian?' Will asked.

Eileen Penrose shook her head. 'Brian knew them. He said they were local scum.'

'You mean they were from Cornwall?'

'Isn't that what I just said?'

Sam forced a smile. He hadn't been sure how much of this investigation he would be allowed to pursue. Even though Penrose was Cornish, he had been killed in Exeter; but if there was a chance his killer was from Cornwall, then it put the ball firmly back in Sam's court. 'Is there anything more you can tell us, Mrs Penrose?'

'Speak to Danny.' This came from Eric Penrose. 'He used to pal about with our boy.'

'That's right,' his wife cut in. 'Danny Santos . . . he went to see Brian in jail a couple of times.'

'Do you know where we can find him?' Sam asked.

'He used to work in Venning's place,' the old man said. 'Reckon that's where you'll find him.'

★ ★ ★

The pet hotel in St Ives turned out to be quirkier than Loveday had imagined. She'd been sceptical of Merrick's insistence that the business wasn't just a creative reinvention of a regular kennels. But she changed her mind when the charismatic owners of the place, Jan and Simon Newman, gave her the conducted tour. It was impressive. Pet beds were lined with sheepskin, special diets were prepared in the stainless steel kitchen, and the on-site 'beauty parlour' turned out perfectly-groomed and -coiffured canine and feline beauties.

Loveday smiled to herself as she drove back to the magazine office. Even if she had a pet, she couldn't see herself calling on the services of the Newmans, but she had no doubt that doting owners would love the place.

It was almost one o'clock when she got back to Truro. She had made notes and recorded the interviews with the Newmans and their staff. She had begun to transcribe them when her phone rang.

'It's me,' Cassie said quickly, before Loveday had a chance to register the name. 'You're late.'

Loveday glanced at the clock. 'Sorry, Cassie. I got involved in something. I'm on my way now.'

Cassie was stirring her second latte and appeared deep in thought when Loveday ran up the stairs to the gallery café to meet her.

'Can I get you another?' she said breathlessly, nodded towards her friend's cup.

Cassie shook her head, and Loveday went to fetch herself a hot chocolate.

'OK, so what's the big mystery?' she said when she got back, pulling out a chair and sitting down.

Cassie frowned. 'Probably nothing, but I just can't get it out of my mind. I didn't think anything of it at the time, but now . . .'

'For goodness' sake, Cassie, stop drawing it out. Just tell me.'

Her friend looked up. 'It's Silas,' she said. 'I think I might know who killed him.'

5

The sun setting over Mounts Bay had turned the sky crimson as Loveday drove along the front in Marazion that evening. The spectacle was too lovely to ignore, so she parked the car at the kitchen door and strolled back along the drive to stand with the growing crowd watching from the beach. Spotting Sam's car coming into the village, she gave him a wave indicating he should join her. A few moments later, they were walking hand in hand across the sand.

'They've come to watch the sunset.' Loveday smiled, nodding to the groups of people all around them.

Sam took a deep breath, drawing in the cool sea air and savouring the crisp sparkle that was all around St Michael's Mount. The setting sun had caught the tiny windows high up on the castle, making them glisten. Loveday took his arm and snuggled her head into his shoulder as they watched the spectacular sunset change the evening sky from pink to mauve, and then to purple. And they stayed watching until darkness began to fall before strolling off the beach, arm in arm.

As they reached the road, Sam smiled down at her. 'I don't suppose there's much to eat at your place?'

Loveday frowned, trying to visualize the contents of her fridge. 'Eggs?'

He laughed. 'That's what I thought. Shall we see what the Godolphin's offering tonight?'

'I thought you'd never ask,' Loveday sighed.

The Godolphin Arms was only a few hundred yards along the front. In the restaurant they found a table overlooking the Mount. Most of the people on the beach had now gone, and from where she sat, Loveday could just make out the outline of the castle in the growing dusk. The waiter brought a wine list, but Sam had no need of it. He ordered a bottle of their favourite Chardonnay, and after a quick scan of the menu they both decided on the chicken curry.

Loveday ate slowly, savouring each tasty mouthful. She knew she had to bring up the Silas Venning investigation, and was anxious to know if Laura really had contacted the police, but she had to choose her moment. It came as she waited for the waiter to bring her homemade apple pie and clotted cream.

She cleared her throat. 'Laura Venning rang me yesterday.'

Sam's head snapped up. He gave her a cautious look, waiting for her to go on.

'She doesn't believe her husband took his own life.' Loveday glanced out over the dark beach, waiting for Sam's response, aware that he was still watching her. When he didn't speak, she said, 'I thought she would ring you.'

He crumbled the remains of his bread roll between his fingers, his lips pressed together.

'Well . . . did she?' Loveday persisted.

Sam released a heartfelt sigh. 'Please tell me you didn't talk her into this.'

Loveday's eyes flew open. 'Talk her into . . . ?' She shook her head in disgust. 'Well, of course I didn't. She rang me.

She wanted to tell me about the holiday they had arranged — and the dental appointment Silas booked the day before he died.' She glared at him, her eyes forcing him to look at her. 'Laura Venning is convinced her husband would never have killed himself, and she thinks the things he had planned are proof of that.'

Sam sat back and let out another long sigh as Loveday went on, 'And a friend of Laura Venning, who just happens to be a doctor, says Silas had a heart condition.'

His eyebrow lifted. Loveday couldn't mistake the warning, so she went on quickly: 'I was there when this doctor, Meredith Deering, called on Laura this morning.' She paused. 'But she only mentioned the heart thing when Laura caught her out in a lie. She said she hadn't seen Silas since the yacht club dance several weeks ago, but that wasn't true.'

She had Sam's attention now. 'Meredith said Silas came to see her unofficially last week, which would make it a couple of days before he died.' Loveday could tell from Sam's expression that he hadn't been aware of this.

Sam shook his head. 'There was nothing at the scene to suggest anything other than suicide,' he said.

Loveday was watching him, saw the blink of his eye, and then she knew. 'You were suspicious too, Sam,' she said, leaning forward.

'You know I can't discuss the case with you.'

'But you are suspicious . . . aren't you?'

He gave her an exasperated look and lifted his hands from the table.

Loveday ran her finger around the rim of her wine glass, not looking at him. 'I'm not the only one who doesn't think Silas Venning did away with himself.' She paused. 'Cassie does, too.'

She darted a glance at him. His expression was grim. Loveday promised herself that she wouldn't bring up Cassie's theory tonight; for that was all it was. But there were parts of it that might be important. Anyway, she had started now, so she had to go on. She cleared her throat.

'You know that Venning Marine has contracted Cassie a couple of times to refurbish some of their older boats?'

Sam waited.

'Well, about six weeks ago she called into their Falmouth yard to check up on some specifications they had supplied, when this chap pushed past her. More like shoved her out of his way, actually.

'Silas Venning's office overlooks the main production floor, so he can see who's doing what, and vice versa. Well, according to Cassie, this guy who'd pushed past her took the stairs to the office two at a time and just kind of threw himself in.

'He grabbed Venning by the throat and would have choked him if a couple of workers hadn't seen what was going on, rushed up the stairs, and pulled him off. In all the confusion that followed, the attacker made off, leaving Venning still struggling for breath.

'Cassie ran up to help. She was ringing for an ambulance when Venning stopped her. He said he was fine and there was no need to involve anyone else. But according to Cassie, he was clutching his throat and apparently in a bad way. When he'd regained his composure he managed to splutter out that the young man was a disgruntled former employee who held a grudge because he had sacked him. He made Cassie promise not to mention the attack to anyone.'

Loveday stopped for a breath, glancing again at Sam. He was interested now. She went on, 'Well, you can imagine how shocked Cassie was, especially since she recognized the guy.'

'She recognized him?' Sam's body tensed.

'Cassie didn't know his name, but she'd seen him working around Falmouth Marina.' She looked up, meeting Sam's stare. 'She reckons that, if anyone murdered Venning, then it was this guy.'

'We won't know if he was murdered, not until the post-mortem results are in,' Sam said. 'Until then, let's just keep an open mind.'

'But you will try to find this man? I mean, it could be important.'

Sam sighed. Loveday Ross could possibly be the most exasperating woman on the planet. Of course they would try to

84

find the man. He was toying with the possibility that this might be the Danny Santos that Eileen Penrose had mentioned — the one who had visited her son in prison. He'd asked one of his team, DC Amanda Fox, to check out the name with Venning Marine. After all, if he worked there they were bound to recognize the name. He was more than suspicious when Amanda reported back that no one at the boatyard was admitting to knowing the man — and the company's record of employees had mysteriously 'disappeared'. Another visit was called for, and this time he'd do it himself.

Sam pushed his plate away and gave Loveday a long look. 'Tell you what,' he said, trying for a tolerant grin, 'I'll go into the magazine office tomorrow and edit the thing, and you can give my team at the nick their instructions for the day.'

'OK, no need for sarcasm. I was only trying to help,' Loveday muttered. But he was still smiling at her, so she gave him a whack with the menu and grinned back. 'I'll be keeping all future information to myself,' she said.

Loveday was good at keeping things to herself, at least until she could evaluate the importance of information. Cassie had told her something else earlier. She'd shared her suspicion that Silas and Meredith Deering were an item. There was nothing definite to go on, she'd said, but the looks she had noticed passing between the couple at the party had made her more than suspicious. Loveday hadn't told Sam about this. She wasn't sure why.

The main street was deserted as they walked slowly back to Loveday's cottage. 'I can't stay tonight,' Sam said, as they walked hand in hand up the drive towards his car.

'Maybe I can persuade you.' Loveday smiled coyly, reaching up to give him a long, lingering kiss on the mouth.

He smoothed her hair away from her face, his voice husky. 'I have an early start in the morning.'

'I have an alarm clock.'

They kissed again, before going into the cottage and closing the door behind them.

★　★　★

Loveday didn't hear Sam leave in the morning, but when she wandered sleepily into the kitchen there was a single yellow rose at the place he'd set for her on the table. She picked it up, touching it to her lips, smiling. She knew it had come from Cassie's garden next door.

The lady herself arrived while Loveday was in the shower. 'Don't worry, I know where the kettle is,' she called through. The rose was sitting in a glass of water when Loveday walked back in, towelling her hair dry. 'Has he moved in, then?' Cassie asked, her smile teasing.

'I'm working on it,' Loveday said.

'Look, I can't stay. I'm on my way to London to meet a client today. I just stopped by to hear the latest on Silas Venning. Did he top himself or not?'

Loveday lifted the mug of coffee her friend had made and sat down. 'As far as Sam is concerned, it's none of my business.' She slid her friend a knowing glance. 'But . . .'

'Yes?' Cassie's eyes were alight with interest.

'I told him your story about the guy

who attacked Venning in his office.'

Cassie stared wide-eyed at her. 'Well, don't keep me in suspense. What did he say? Does he think this man could have killed Silas?' Her hand flew to her mouth. 'I've just had a thought. What if he recognized me that day too? Oh God, Loveday. What if he comes after Adam and the kids?'

Loveday put down her coffee and went to put a reassuring arm around her friend. 'Of course that won't happen. He probably didn't recognize you. If Venning didn't make an issue of it at the time, then this guy has probably forgotten all about it by now.'

'So you don't think he killed Silas?'

That was one question Loveday definitely couldn't answer. She went back to her drink. She said, 'If Silas *was* murdered, then I imagine there will be plenty of candidates out there. You don't run a business like that without picking up a few enemies along the way.'

Cassie nodded. 'I suppose you're right. It's just that, when I thought about this incident it seemed so important. I'm not even sure it *was* anymore.'

'Well, there you are then,' Loveday said. 'And as far as what Sam thinks about it . . . I honestly have no idea, but I expect you will get a visit.'

Cassie glanced at her watch. 'It'll have to be tomorrow, then. I don't know what time I'll get back.'

'I'll let him know,' Loveday said, as she went in search of her bag, and fished out the newspaper cutting she'd printed out the day before, smoothing it on the table. 'How does this strike you for another theory? Silas and the glamorous doctor he's draping himself all over here were having an affair.'

Cassie's eyebrows went up. 'Were they?'

'Well, it was your idea, Cassie. I know it's just a theory, but if they were, and . . . ' She tapped the cutting. ' . . . Laura here got to know about it? Well, don't you think that would be a reason to kill her husband?'

'What? Kill your old man because he was having a bit of rumpy-pumpy? Isn't that a bit far-fetched?'

Loveday grinned. 'Wouldn't you kill

Adam if he behaved like that?'

'Dead right I would,' Cassie said. 'But I'm an evil bitch. Laura Venning is a *lady*.' She emphasized the word with a chortle.

Loveday shook her head, laughing. 'You might be incorrigible, Cassie, but you're far from being an evil bitch; and I suspect our Laura is not as much of a lady as she would have us believe. Besides, it's her who's insisting that Silas was murdered. She would hardly throw suspicion on herself, would she?'

'So we're back to square one,' Cassie sighed, getting up and heading for the back door.

6

There was a message from Laura Venning waiting for Loveday when she arrived at the office. The woman said she wanted her help and wanted to see her. Loveday was thoughtful as she drove to Trevore, and more than curious about what had prompted this latest invitation. There was no getting away from the fact that Silas's death was a mystery, and although Loveday itched to get involved, she felt guilty for even considering it.

She had been keeping an eye on a blue Metro just ahead of her when the driver indicated she was pulling out to pass a slower-moving lorry. Loveday followed suit. The car slowed when it reached the turn-off to Trevore, and the indicator flicked briefly on again. Loveday's foot touched the brake, expecting the car to make the turn, but it didn't. Evidently the driver had changed her mind. Loveday didn't recognize the car, although there was something familiar about the long blonde hair.

She thought no more about the incident as she followed the winding road to the Venning mansion. Laura must have been watching for her, for as Loveday pulled up and parked at the side of the house, the woman was standing by the open front door. She wore black tailored trousers and a pale grey silk blouse tucked in at the waist, with a single row of pearls at her throat.

She held her arms wide, drawing Loveday into the house, leading her through to the big front room. 'I'm so glad you could come,' she said, indicating one of the two large sofas. 'Can I get you a drink?' Her eyes went to the bottle-laden table behind the sofa. 'Or maybe you would prefer a cup of tea.'

Loveday smiled. 'I'm fine . . . really. Your message said something about wanting my help?'

Laura lifted a drink she had already poured for herself. 'You're busy. I can see that. I'm . . . ' She hesitated. 'It's just that there's somewhere I have to go, and I don't want to go there on my own.'

'Go where?'

'To Bolger's Wood.'

Loveday stared at her, shaking her head. 'I'm not sure that's a good idea, Laura.'

Laura tilted her chin, staring past Loveday to the river. Her voice sounded shaky. 'I have to go,' she went on. 'I have to see the place where Silas died.'

Loveday sighed. This was exactly what everyone had warned her against. 'Wouldn't you rather go with one of your family . . . your mother, perhaps? I'm assuming that she and your father are back from their cruise?'

'Yes, they're back.' She moistened her lips with the tip of her tongue. 'My mother is the last person I would want with me. She would think it was freaky to want to go out there.'

'Your doctor friend, then . . . '

'Meredith! Heavens, no. I think she's done enough.'

Loveday shook her head. 'I don't understand.'

'She lied to me, didn't she?' Laura

raised her voice. 'I can't trust her anymore.'

Loveday got up and went to the window. She could see someone fishing on the far bank of the river, and wondered if he'd caught anything. She knew she should walk away, but Laura did seem to need her help. And although she was trying to ignore it, there was a growing curl of curiosity at the pit of her stomach.

★ ★ ★

Silas Venning — or the person who killed him — could hardly have chosen a more inaccessible place for the deed. They'd been driving for more than a mile along a rough track before they came to Bolger's Wood. Loveday pulled into a clearing and frowned into the dense undergrowth. 'What do we do now? Is this what you came to see?'

'I want to walk,' Laura said, getting out of the car. She had changed into a grey tracksuit and trainers.

Loveday looked down at her new black

patent leather shoes, and grimaced. 'If that's what you want.'

There was a track of sorts and they took it, advancing in single file slowly through the tangle of branches. The further they penetrated into the wood, the darker it became. Loveday pushed her hair out of her eyes and squinted into the gloom. 'I don't think we should go any further.' She glanced behind her. 'I'm not even sure we can find our way back from here.'

Laura turned suddenly, desperation flashing in her dark eyes. 'We haven't come to the tree yet.'

How could Laura possibly know the exact tree where — ? Loveday froze. Had the woman been here when Silas died? A sickening chill was beginning to seep through her. There was a clearing ahead, and she could see the blue-and-white police tape fluttering.

'We're here,' Laura said, stooping to duck under the tape. Apart from the two of them, the place was deserted. And there had been no signs of any police activity on the way in to this spot.

Loveday followed Laura's stare to a sturdy oak, a thick branch poking out at right angles. She swallowed hard. 'How did you know which tree it would be, Laura?'

'Because this is our tree. It could only have happened here.' Laura moved forward and stretched out a hand, flattening it against the trunk. 'We found it one day when we were walking. Look . . . ' Her finger traced the outline of a rough carving. 'Silas traced our initials, T and I — Tristan and Isolde, our pet names for each other.'

Loveday peered at the carving. The police were bound to have spotted this, but they wouldn't have connected them to the dead man, not when the initials were so different from the couple's actual names. It was still something Sam should be told about. If it was only Silas and Laura who knew about this place, then surely he had to have killed himself?

Laura was watching her. 'You're thinking this proves that Silas did commit suicide.'

Loveday's shoulders lifted. 'I'm so

sorry, Laura, but I can't see any other explanation now. No-one else could have known how special this tree was to both of you.'

'We don't know that,' Laura snapped back. 'How do we know that Silas didn't tell anyone?'

Loveday gave another shrug. 'It's not the kind of thing you would tell anyone else about. I mean . . . it was only special to you two.'

'Well, someone knew,' Laura said bitterly. 'And that someone killed him.'

They drove back to Trevore House in silence. There was a shiny black Mercedes in the drive. 'My parents,' Laura announced flatly. 'Do you mind if I don't invite you in? I don't want my mother to know where we've been.' She hesitated. 'She wouldn't understand.'

Loveday smiled and put a hand on Laura's arm. 'I wasn't much help, was I?'

Laura looked up, her eyes slits. 'Silas was murdered, and I'm going to prove it.' She stepped out of the car, slamming the door behind her, and didn't look back.

Loveday sighed as she restarted the

engine. So much for wanting to help the woman. She'd made matters worse.

All the way back to the magazine office, she was steeling herself to tell Sam what she'd learned that morning. But when she got back to her desk, before she had a chance to make the call, he rang her.

'I don't suppose you're free for a drink?' he said.

Loveday hesitated. She didn't really want to pass on this new information in a public place. She'd no idea how he would react . . . well, apart from criticizing her for poking her nose in when she'd promised not to. But she had important new information for him. He *should* be pleased.

'Nothing fancy,' he went on. 'I was thinking maybe a tuna sandwich and a pint at the Crab and Creel.'

She nodded at the phone. 'Sounds great, Sam. I'll see you there in half an hour.'

She was still thoughtful, cradling the phone on her shoulder long after he broke the connection. She didn't notice Merrick walking over to her desk, and started when he spoke.

'I'll walk with you,' he said.

Loveday's head shot up. 'What?'

'To the pub. I take it that was Sam?'

'Well, yes, but . . . '

'He's invited me along, too. He didn't tell you?'

Loveday shook her head. So this wasn't to be a cosy drink for two. But she was already feeling better that she didn't have to face Sam alone.

He was standing at the bar with his back to them when they walked in. Despite herself, Loveday felt a rush of pleasure at the sight of him. When he turned and saw them, his face split into a smile, and Loveday realized again how handsome he was. He nodded to an empty table. 'Grab that one, Loveday. I've ordered a glass of white for you. Is that OK?'

She nodded her approval and slid into a window seat. She could see the cathedral from here. One of the towers was still encased in scaffolding. She had already arranged with the architect of the refurbishment work to publish an article once the project was completed.

Loveday looked up and smiled when

she saw Merrick approaching. He put her wine on the table and slid in beside her. 'What's all the cloak and dagger stuff about, Merrick? Has Sam said anything?'

'He's got the PM report on Silas Venning,' Merrick said.

'Ah.' She felt a twinge of unease. She would definitely have to tell Sam now that she'd been to Bolger's Wood with Laura. He wasn't going to be pleased. She waited for him to join them, and watched as he slid two pint glasses onto the table. 'Merrick says you've had the post-mortem results?'

Sam arranged his glass on a well-used beer mat and glanced around the bar, making sure none of the other customers was within earshot. He didn't want what he was going to tell them to be made public . . . not yet, anyway.

Loveday frowned. 'Well . . . ?'

He sighed. 'You were right. Silas didn't kill himself.'

She sank back into her seat, staring at him. All she could think was that she and Laura had been tramping about in what was surely now a crime scene, possibly even destroying evidence. She cleared her throat. 'You mean he was dead before the rope was put round his neck?'

'Not exactly,' Sam said. 'Bartholomew found bruising on the neck just at the carotid artery. Here . . . ' He placed a finger on his own neck to demonstrate. 'Pressure applied to this point would render a person unconscious.' He reached for his pint and took a long drink, wiping the foam from his mouth with the back of his hand.

Merrick slid his spectacles back up his nose. 'That would suggest the killer had some medical knowledge, wouldn't it?'

Medical! Suddenly, it clicked in Loveday's head. That was it. The scene that had happened earlier that morning when she'd been on her way to Laura's house was scrolling through her mind. She could see the blue Metro in the road ahead of her, and the female driver dithering about whether or not to turn off. She'd thought at the time that there was something familiar about the long blonde hair. Now she knew. The driver was Meredith Deering — Doctor Meredith Deering, who would know all about carotid arteries.

Merrick and Sam were staring at her. 'Is there something I should know?' Sam asked, his brow furrowing.

'Well, no . . . it's just that I met Laura's doctor friend, Meredith Deering, at her house yesterday I told you about it.' She glanced up, locking eyes with him. 'You said the killer would be someone with medical knowledge.'

Sam shook his head. 'Not necessarily. Anyone can search the Internet for that kind of information.' He was still studying her face. 'What do you know about Dr Deering?'

Loveday grimaced. She'd liked the woman, and was now regretting ever mentioning her. From what Sam had just said, she could have absolutely nothing to do with all this. There was no way such a slightly-built woman could have heaved an unconscious man up on to that branch.

But she had lied to Laura about having seen Silas. If they were as close friends as Laura had suggested, surely Meredith would have mentioned his illness? She thought again about the blue Metro. Why had Meredith changed her mind about visiting Laura? Loveday reached for her wine glass and was surprised to find it was empty.

'I'll get you another,' Merrick said, getting up and heading for the bar. Aware that Sam was still watching her, Loveday took a deep breath, and described her meeting with the attractive young doctor. When she got to the bit about Silas's heart condition, Sam frowned. 'There was nothing about a heart condition in the PM report.'

'Are you sure?'

Sam raised an eyebrow, and Loveday recognized the warning. The post-mortem stuff would hardly be wrong. So why had the doctor lied? And then she knew!

'What?' Sam said impatiently.

Loveday paused before speaking. 'I don't know anything for sure. It's just that Cassie mentioned something the other day. At the time I dismissed it as gossip, but now I'm not so sure.'

Sam let out an exasperated sigh. 'For heaven's sake, Loveday, stop beating about the bush and just tell me.'

She cleared her throat. 'Cassie thought Silas and Meredith were having a fling.'

Sam sucked in his bottom lip. 'Did she, now? And why would she think that?'

'She's done some work on his yacht.' She hesitated, wondering if she was even remembering this correctly. 'She'd seen the whole crowd of them together, and got the impression that Silas and Meredith were more than just friends.' She paused, taking another deep breath. 'Actually, Sam, there's something else I need to tell you.'

He waited, saying nothing. Loveday glanced round. She could see Merrick still waiting at the bar to be served. She didn't want him to hear this. 'Laura and I were out there this morning . . . at Bolger's Wood.'

Sam stared at her. He put up his hand. 'Please don't tell me you contaminated a murder scene, Loveday?'

'But it wasn't a murder scene,' she hissed. 'At least, not when we were out there.'

'You didn't see the police tape, then?'

It was Loveday's turn to raise her hand.

'I'm sorry, Sam. I don't know what else to say.'

Sam gave a long, heartfelt sigh. 'You can start by telling me what the two of you were doing there.'

'It was Laura's idea. The place was special to her and Silas.' She shrugged. 'I suppose she just wanted to see where he died.'

Sam frowned. 'Special?'

Loveday nodded. 'It was *their* tree, you see. They used to go there when they were courting. Silas carved their initials into the bark.'

Sam was trying to remember the details of what he had seen when he was at the site. Everyone had assumed it was a suicide . . . everyone but him. He hadn't wanted to admit it, but he hadn't been happy about it. It had struck him that Silas Venning was too busy making money to kill himself. He'd seen the rough initials carved into the trunk and had instructed the police photographer to take pictures of them. 'As far as I can remember, the initials were T and I.'

'That's right.' Loveday nodded. 'Tristan

and Isolde. They were the couple's pet names for each other — lovers from medieval legend, I think. But you're missing the point. Why did the killer choose that particular tree? I mean, how would they even know about it?'

As far as Sam was concerned, it left the grieving widow right bang in the frame. But could it be that easy? 'If we rule Laura out of it, who else knew about the significance of that tree?' He was hardly aware that he'd spoken aloud.

'Well, that's just it,' Loveday said. 'According to Laura, no one knew. And it couldn't have been her, because then she wouldn't have taken me there. It would have been too obvious.'

'Silas could have told someone,' Sam said.

Merrick had returned with a tray of drinks and put it on the table. He eyed them with suspicion. 'Have I missed something?'

Sam met Loveday's eyes. 'Will you tell him, or shall I?'

'Good lunch?' Keri asked, as Loveday and Merrick walked back into the office.

'Working lunch,' Loveday answered, sitting down at her computer. One of the first things she had done when Merrick took her on as his editor was to rearrange the desks by pushing hers and Keri's together so they could work facing each other. 'Any calls while I was out?' she asked.

Keri flicked over the page of her notebook. 'A Dr Deering rang. She wants you to call her back.' She scribbled down a number and handed it across. Loveday took the note, her brow wrinkling as she stared at it. It was a local landline number, probably her extension at the hospital. 'Did she say what she wanted?'

'Only that it was important she should speak to you.'

Loveday was already punching the number into her mobile. It rang out, and then a woman answered.

'Dr Deering?' Loveday said. 'You wanted to speak to me?'

'Oh, Miss Ross. I . . . er . . . yes. Can we meet?'

Loveday reached for her diary, flicking over the pages. She had scheduled a telephone interview with a young woman who had set up a new surfing business, and she also had a meeting with two of the magazine's freelance contributors to discuss possible future articles. 'I'm afraid it will have to be tomorrow.'

There was a pause at the other end of the line, and then Meredith Deering said, 'I could come to your home tonight, if it wouldn't be putting you out too much?' She sounded agitated.

Loveday ran a hand over her hair, pushing it away from her face. 'You sound worried, Meredith. Is everything all right?'

'What? Well, yes of course it is.' The assurance came quickly . . . too quickly. Loveday wondered if it had anything to do with Sam contacting her. If he turned up at the cottage tonight and found Meredith there . . . She bit her lip. She was already in his bad books. No doubt he would see any contact with the doctor as more interference on her part.

She glanced back to the diary. 'If it's

that urgent, I'll rearrange one of my appointments. Do you know the museum in Truro? There's a café — '

'I know it,' Meredith interrupted.

'Can you get there in half an hour?' Loveday didn't have long to wait for confirmation. 'OK, see you there,' she said. She clicked off the connection and glanced at Keri. 'Can you reschedule that Katie Ransome interview for four-thirty today?'

Keri nodded, her hand already hovering over the phone.

Loveday fired up the article she had started to write earlier and began tapping her keyboard. She wasn't on deadline for it, but she had to produce at least some work that day if she was going to meet the magazine's copy targets. She glanced across to Merrick's office and saw he was on the phone. She wondered if it was Sam he was talking to.

* * *

The smell of freshly-made coffee greeted Loveday as soon as she walked into the

109

museum café. Meredith was already there. She caught her eye and waved. The woman stood up, offering her hand. 'Thanks so much for coming.'

Loveday sat down and gave what she hoped was an encouraging smile.

Meredith looked uneasy. 'You must be wondering what this is all about?' she said.

Loveday waited.

'I lied about Silas having a heart condition,' Meredith said, moistening her lips. 'Well, I didn't exactly lie; it was what he told me. I wasn't his GP, so it could have been true. I should have explained things better, it was stupid. I just panicked when Laura asked when I'd last seen him.' She looked away.

'Go on,' Loveday said.

The woman forced herself to look at Loveday. 'I knew the post-mortem would catch me out.' She paused. 'I suppose your policeman friend has already told you that.'

'My policeman friend?' How did Meredith Deering know about her and Sam?

'Detective Inspector Kitto. Oh . . . ' she said, putting a hand to her mouth. 'Was I not supposed to know about that?'

'Hang on a minute,' Loveday said. 'Know about what? Who told you that Sam and I were friends?'

'Laura. She didn't mean to, it just kind of slipped out.'

Loveday sat back in her chair. So Laura Venning *did* know about her and Sam? It wasn't exactly a secret, but how would she know?

'I'm sorry; I'm getting confused here,' she said. 'Why did you lie about Silas being ill?'

Meredith swallowed. 'Silas and I were . . . ' She hesitated. 'We were close.'

'You were having an affair?'

Meredith gave a reluctant nod. 'It just happened,' she said. 'Silas was very persuasive. I felt terrible about it. Laura is my best friend.'

'Did Laura know about the affair?'

Meredith stared at her, wide-eyed. 'Of course she didn't. That's why I was panicked into lying. It would tear her apart, especially now that he's . . . '

Loveday sighed. 'You do realize that there is no way you can keep this a secret now? It's all going to come out, Meredith. It has to.' A thought suddenly struck her. 'That place where Silas died . . . did you know it?'

Meredith nodded miserably. 'Bolger's Wood. We used to meet there. There was this big oak tree where other lovers had carved messages to each other. It was our special place.'

So Laura wasn't the only person who knew about the tree. Loveday wondered how many other woman Silas had taken there. In some ways, meeting at that tree was an even greater betrayal of Laura than the infidelity.

She was still going over the conversation in her mind as she left the office that evening. The worst of the teatime traffic was over, so there were no queues at the main city roundabout. She glanced back as she drove past the ugly grey building that was the area headquarters of the Devon and Cornwall Constabulary, and wondered if Sam was still inside.

Normally she took the high road out of

the city, but this evening Loveday had a lot to think about. She hadn't been surprised about the affair between Meredith and Silas, but Laura knowing all about her relationship with Sam — well, that *did* startle her. If the woman was assuming everything they discussed was being reported back to the police, it put the whole thing a different light . . . unless, of course, Meredith was lying again. She'd already proved she was capable of that. But Loveday didn't think so. If her career in journalism had taught her anything, it was to spot when she was being spun a yarn.

She tried to straighten out the facts. Meredith was a doctor — and she was having an affair with her best friend's husband. Why would she kill her lover? Had Silas threatened to tell Laura about their relationship? She shook her head. That was hardly likely.

By the time she reached Marazion, her head was buzzing. She drove along the seafront, smiling to herself at how peaceful it all was in the early evening. The sun was beginning to set across the bay, above the rooftops of Penzance, sending the familiar pink cloudy streaks across the sky. It made her feel wistful, remembering how she and Sam had watched the exact same scene the evening before.

The tide was out, and Loveday could see a vehicle crossing the causeway to St Michael's Mount. Lights were beginning to come on in the houses over at the tiny harbour as she turned into her drive.

Cassie had been watching for her car and came to the kitchen door, wiping her hands on her apron as Loveday pulled up. 'I need to talk to you. I've been feeling bad about something all day.'

Loveday got out of the car and smiled at her friend. 'You'd better come in, then.'

Cassie followed her into the kitchen. Loveday glanced to the kettle. 'What's it to be . . . a cup of tea or a glass of white?'

Cassie flopped into a chair. 'Adam's putting the monsters to bed, so I'll have a glass of wine . . . if you're going to join me.'

Loveday shrugged. She dismissed thoughts of the wine she'd already had at lunch-time. 'Why not? I think we both deserve it.' She took a couple of glasses from the cupboard and found an unopened bottle in the fridge and began to pour. She held the glass out to Cassie. 'OK, so what's this terrible thing that you've done?'

'It's been on the news. The police are treating Silas Venning's death as suspicious. Is that the same thing as murder?'

'It's exactly what it suggests, Cassie. They're suspicious about the circumstances surrounding his death.' It wasn't up to her to say Silas had been murdered.

Cassie laughed. 'You're beginning to sound like Sam.'

'Am I?' Loveday winced. 'I don't mean to. Anyway, what's all this about?'

Cassie sat down at the table and fiddled with the stem of her wine glass. Loveday waited.

Eventually, Cassie said, 'I hope you didn't tell Sam what I said about that nice young woman doctor. It was all gossip, you know; I was just repeating gossip. I've really no idea if she was having a fling with Silas Venning.' She frowned. 'Adam's furious with me. He thinks I might have got the doctor into trouble.'

Loveday shook her head. 'You can relax. You didn't speak out of turn. As it happens, you were right. Meredith told me herself that she and Silas were having an affair.'

Cassie stared at her. 'And the police know about this?'

Loveday nodded. 'They do.'

Cassie put her glass down and let out a long sigh. 'Well, at least I haven't been telling tales out of school, so that's a relief. After Adam's reaction, I've been worrying about it all day.'

'Does Adam know Meredith Deering well?'

'He's met her at the hospital when he's been calling in to see one or other of his patients. He said she's a really sweet person.'

Cassie caught sight of the clock and jumped up, downing the rest of her wine in one go. 'I'd better get back before our adorable children drown their father.'

Loveday smiled as she watched her go. She'd been so lucky finding this little cottage and renting it from Cassie and Adam. They were more than her landlords and neighbours, they were like family.

It had grown dark while they'd been talking, and she got up to switch on the lights, suddenly realizing how hungry she was. She checked the fridge. She still hadn't managed to get to the supermarket, but there were a few salad things in there. She fished out a couple of pork chops from the freezer and set them aside to defrost in the microwave. She had no idea whether Sam would appear at her door tonight. He was probably still annoyed with her for contaminating his crime scene — and he was right to be. She should have known better. It would serve her right if he decided never to speak to her again, let alone . . .

She didn't finish her train of thought, because then she heard his car coming up the drive, and hurried to the door to greet him.

7

Cassie's Land Rover was parked in the drive as Sam left Loveday's cottage the following morning. She must have arrived back from London late the previous night, or in the early hours. Either way, he didn't think she would appreciate being called on for an interview at this hour, but speaking to Cassie was at the top of Sam's list of priorities for the day. Loveday had mentioned how busy she was with the current refurbishment of a yacht in Falmouth Marina, and he guessed she wouldn't leave it too late to get there.

It was mid-morning when he and Will drove into the town and parked up at the marina. The *White Dancer* wasn't difficult to find. Even amongst the most glamorous of vessels it stood out, not least because it appeared to be buzzing with activity. Someone on deck was using a power tool, noise competing with the sound of hammering from somewhere below. Sam and Will watched with some amusement as a young man attempted to negotiate a large bolt of black leather upholstery down into the cabin. Once the way was clear, they were about to step down onto the deck when Cassie, a clipboard tucked under her arm, appeared from inside the cabin.

She stopped in her tracks, surprised when she saw Sam. 'What on earth are you doing here?' She clamped a hand to her mouth. 'It's not Loveday, is it? Has something happened?'

'No, Loveday's fine.' Sam laughed, raising a hand in reassurance. 'It's you we've come to see.'

Cassie's puzzled frown changed to a worried one as the realization dawned. 'You've come about Silas Venning?'

Sam nodded.

Cassie glanced back at the *White Dancer*. 'We can't talk here. There's a tearoom just outside the marina. We can go there.'

The two detectives followed her back along the boardwalk and through the security gate to a small wooden hut displaying a sign for 'Teas and Coffees'. Cassie led the way inside and selected one of the half-dozen small tables. None of them were occupied.

Will went up and ordered three teas, and came back balancing them on a tin tray. When they were all settled, he slipped a notebook from his coat pocket and searched his other pockets for a pen.

'Can you repeat to us what you told Loveday?' Sam said.

Ten minutes later, Will had filled four pages of his notebook.

Sam said, 'I don't suppose you know this man's name?'

Cassie looked embarrassed. 'Sorry, Sam, but I could describe him if that's any help.'

Sam nodded and said that it would be.

Cassie cupped her hands around her cooling tea. 'Let me see. He's about five-eleven, slight build, blond curly hair, piercing blue eyes. I've seen him around the marina here, working on some of the yachts.'

'When — before what happened — was the last time you saw him?' Sam asked.

'Probably a few weeks before the

incident at Venning Marine. He was doing some work on the *Magpie*.' She nodded towards the marina. 'It's the white cruiser over there at the end of the boardwalk.'

Sam and Will glanced out in the direction she'd indicated.

'But you won't find anyone there, if that's what you were thinking,' Cassie told them. 'It's owned by a London couple, and they only ever come down at weekends.'

Sam nodded, making a mental note for one of his team to interview the couple. He stood up and offered his hand. 'Thanks, Cassie, you've been a great help.'

The woman behind the counter watched them leave. She'd heard snatches of the conversation, and was now reaching for the phone.

As the detectives walked slowly back to their car, Will said, 'Do you really think this guy might have something to do with Venning's death?'

No idea,' Sam said, 'but Penrose's mother mentioned him too. And he did go to see him in prison. I think we need to rattle a few cages at Venning Marine.'

The boatyard was on the other side of Falmouth. Sam could see a collection of white masts bobbing to the side of the building as they approached; and, judging by the level of activity around the area, the loss of Silas Venning hadn't stopped business progressing as usual. Sam spotted an empty space in the busy car park and pulled into it.

He and Will made their way to the reception, pulling out their ID cards to show the middle-aged woman behind the desk. 'We'd like to speak to the person in charge,' Sam said.

The woman glanced at the cards with a sour expression, and then back to the two detectives. 'If you wait here, I will try to find someone for you,' she said, disappearing out the back of the tiny office.

Sam and Will didn't wait. They followed the sound of a power drill and sawing activity into what appeared to be the yard's main work floor. A couple of men were planing down the wooden shell of a boat while another worked a jigsaw, his head bent in concentration over his task. The smells of new wood and varnish, coupled with the sound of power tools, told Sam that more work activities were going on in other corners of the vast place. He had his reservations about Venning Marine, but at least the workforce seemed to be industrious.

Glancing up to the windows of the elevated office, he could see the snooty woman from reception through the glass. She was talking to a tall, blond man, who had the sleeves of his immaculate white shirt rolled up. Sam and Will made their way up the stairs and walked uninvited into the office.

They pulled out their warrant cards again and showed them to the man.

'And you are, sir?' Sam enquired.

The receptionist tutted. 'I told them to wait downstairs, Mr Barnes.'

'It's fine, Eleanor. I'll attend to these officers now.'

The woman shook her head, flashing a disdainful glance in Sam and Will's direction before scuttling off down the stairs and back to her domain in the reception office.

'You must forgive Eleanor. She's very

protective of us. She's been with us a long time.' The man came forward extending his hand. 'I'm Liam Barnes,' he said. 'Acting Director of Venning Marine. Please take a seat.'

The detectives remained standing as Sam took time to note the expensively-cut hair, the toned body, the easy, confident way the man moved. A touch too confident, perhaps? There was a hint of wariness in the blue-grey eyes.

'We've come about the death of Silas Venning,' Sam launched in without ceremony. 'Can you tell us when you last saw Mr Venning?'

Liam Barnes gave Sam a sharp look. 'I don't understand. Silas took his own life. Why exactly are you here? Surely you know no one else was involved in this tragedy?'

'Can you just answer the question, Mr Barnes?'

Liam Barnes glanced uneasily down to the shop floor, where curious looks were being directed at the two officers.

'Last Friday, it would have been,' he said, without looking back at Sam. 'We left the yard together around six o'clock.'

'You didn't go for a drink?'

'No.' Barnes turned and met Sam's eyes. 'We sometimes did have a pint together in the Greenlawns Hotel, but that was usually if there had been work glitches, things that needed ironing out. Silas believed the mind was more receptive to problems in a relaxed atmosphere.'

'So there were problems?' Will picked up.

'Every company has its ups and downs.' Liam Barnes' gaze slid back to the activities going on below.

Sam nodded to the floor below. 'It all looks busy enough to me.'

'Believe it or not, Inspector, what you see down there is the construction of one new yacht, and some repairs to another. We need to be working on at least three new orders to keep afloat.' Barnes gave a grim smile. 'If you'll excuse the pun.'

He had been standing with his back to them, surveying the activities below. He suddenly squared his shoulders and spun round to face the detectives. 'All right, you might as well know. Venning Marine is going through a bad patch. Orders are drying up, and we were having to let a few people go.'

'How serious is it?' Sam asked. He was beginning to wonder if Silas Venning could have taken his own life after all. If his business was failing and he was in debt . . . He let the thought linger in his head.

'Well, the bank wasn't about to foreclose on the company's loan, if that's what you mean. Besides, Silas didn't have far to look when he was short of cash.' He paused, worried that he was now speaking out of turn. But it was obvious from the expressions of interest on the faces of the two police officers that he wouldn't be allowed to leave it at that.

'Silas's wife is independently wealthy, and her parents are Graham and Geraldine Anstey.'

Sam had to think for a moment to remind himself who this couple was, and then it clicked. Anstey, the property developers, who had a reputation for snapping up large, run-down buildings and turning them into million-pound residences. The company's slogan flashed into his mind: *Elegant homes for the discerning buyer.*

'I don't understand,' Sam said. 'If it would have been as simple as you suggest for Mr Venning to go to his wife for financial backing, why was there a cash flow problem?'

'And why was there a bank loan in the first place?' Will threw in.

Barnes shrugged. 'Who knows what goes on in other people's marriages? Maybe he did ask Laura to invest in the business and she refused. Like I said, I just don't know. But Silas was worried about something, and if it wasn't the business, then it was something else.'

'Do you have a financial interest in the business, Mr Barnes?' Sam asked.

The man shook his head. 'I used to, but Silas bought me out. He still regarded me as a partner, even though I'm just the workhorse around here.'

'But you're acting director,' Will intervened.

'In name only. 'Works foreman' would

be a more accurate description these days.'

The man was looking supremely confident again. He was no works foreman, not if Sam was any judge of people. He said, 'Can you just explain something for me, Mr Barnes? This company builds luxury yachts, and — correct me if I'm wrong — sells them for millions.'

'Ah, well, that's just the problem,' Liam Barnes cut in. 'We haven't been selling too many yachts lately. The wealthy like their little luxuries, but if they can get the same thing cheaper elsewhere, then that's where they will go.'

He moved across to his desk and picked up a pen, twirling it between his fingers. 'Things have been going badly for Silas since Michael Clayton took on a new partner. James Barratt has turned a sleepy little boatyard in Penzance into a force to be reckoned with. They've been undercutting us, grabbing our business from right under our noses.'

Something about the man's arrogance set Sam's teeth on edge. Venning Marine might be a failing company, but Liam Barnes was a man going places — and didn't he know it. It crossed Sam's mind that Liam might have already been headhunted by the Penzance company, but he continued to pursue his line of questioning. 'Surely a business like Venning Marine can be no stranger to competition? Cornwall is full of boat-yards, and they all seem to survive somehow. Why does another one make all that much difference?'

'Clayton-Barratt have been doing more than just competing. They have been deliberately targeting our customers, slashing their prices, and even enticing away our workforce by dangling carrots of higher wages.'

He looked up. 'They are out to destroy us, Inspector — and they're doing a good job. So if you are looking for a reason why Silas would have wanted to take his own life, you have it right there.'

Sam looked out over the wooden frame of a boat under construction. The workers had lost interest in them now, and had returned to their chores. The picture Liam Barnes was carefully painting of his late partner was that of a loser. It wasn't the image Sam had of the man. Silas Venning had the reputation of being a hard man, a business tycoon who could be as ruthless as any when required. He was also a well-known ladies' man.

He turned to Barnes. 'We won't take up any more of your time for the moment, sir, but I would be grateful if you could call into the police station in Truro and give a statement.'

The smooth façade of Liam Barnes slipped. 'Why on earth do I need to give a statement?' He almost spat out the words. 'I've told you everything I know.'

'We could take you back with us now, if that's more convenient for you, sir.' Will's smile was more mischievous than helpful.

'No. I'll make my own arrangements,' Barnes said sharply.

As they turned to leave, Sam stopped suddenly, spun round. 'Just one more thing. Can you remember an incident a few weeks ago when Mr Venning was attacked here in this office?'

Barnes flushed. 'No, sorry.'

'Well, Silas wasn't on his own at the time. I thought the person with him might have been you?'

Barnes shook his head — a little too quickly, Sam thought.

'It wasn't me,' Barnes snapped. 'I don't know anything about it.'

Sam nodded. 'Do you know Danny Santos?'

'Who? Er . . . no.' But he had hesitated long enough for Sam to know he was lying.

'And are you still claiming you didn't see the attack on Silas Venning?'

Liam Barnes glared at Sam. 'I'm not *claiming* anything. I've already told you, I wasn't here when it happened.'

'But you would have been told about it,' Sam persisted. 'Your boss being attacked here in his office could hardly have been an everyday occurrence.'

'Of course I knew about it,' Barnes snapped. 'But, like I said, I wasn't here when it happened.'

'I understand it wasn't reported to the police,' Will said. 'Wasn't that a little unusual?'

'It would have been Silas's decision. I've no idea why he didn't report it.'

Sam held the man's arrogant gaze for a

few seconds longer than he needed to before nodding and thanking him.

He could feel Barnes' eyes on his back as he and Will walked down the stairs and made their way back to their car. Liam Barnes had actually helped their investigation, but maybe not in the way he had intended.

Sam was smiling as he and Will made their way back to the car park. They had succeeded in cracking Liam Barnes' tough veneer. He was already looking forward to their next visit to Venning Marine.

'I need a word,' a course voice rasped, as a man with the girth of an all-in wrestler, and an expression to match, emerged from behind a parked car.

'And who would you be?' Sam asked, giving the newcomer a hard stare.

'I suppose Barnes dropped the Penzance lot in it?'

'Excuse me,' Will interrupted. 'But who exactly are you?'

'That doesn't matter,' the Giant Haystacks-esque man grunted. 'I'm just telling you not to believe him. He's got it in for them up the road. They're not the ones that topped the old bugger.' He flicked puffy, red-rimmed eyes back to the boatyard. 'Your lot don't need to look no further than in there.'

'If you have information about Silas Venning's death, I think you need to come back to the station with us.'

Will opened the back door of the car, indicating that the Great Man-Mountain should get in. But the big guy pulled back.

'I'm going nowhere wi' you.'

'We're not asking you,' Sam said. 'Just get in the car.' He held the man's aggressive stare, hoping there wasn't going to be trouble. If the situation deteriorated into violence, the two of them would be no match for the man. Sam stood his ground. The man hesitated, glanced back to Venning Marine boatyard, then ducked his head and squeezed his bulk into the back seat.

*　*　*

Loveday had given Sam her word that she would steer clear of the police

133

investigation into Silas Venning's death. Everyone was right: it had nothing to do with her. Her workload for the day was so heavy anyway that there was little time for anything else. There were two major articles to edit, an editorial meeting, and a trip to the publishers to tie up any loose ends before the current edition of the magazine went to press.

Loveday was exhausted as she drove home that night. She had been hoping to find Sam waiting for her at the cottage, but it was in darkness as she pulled up.

By contrast, lights blazed from almost every window in Cassie and Adam's house. Loveday smiled as the excited squeals of the couple's two children drifted across the yard. She stood for a moment, listening, trying to imagine what kind of mother she would have made if her life had taken a different path. She didn't have to be a career woman all her life. Maybe she and Sam . . . ? Loveday shook her head at the fanciful thought that had flitted through her mind, and let herself into the cottage.

* * *

Merrick Tremayne glanced up from his desk as Loveday walked into the office next morning, and beckoned her in. The glass panel that separated his office from the rest of the editorial floor gave him the advantage of being able to see what each member of his team was up to at a glance. Loveday slipped off her black leather jacket and slid it onto a hanger on the coat stand before tapping lightly on Merrick's door. He beckoned her in, took off his spectacles, and inclined his head for her to sit.

Without preamble, he said, 'I'm not happy about running this Venning article. The magazine could be seen as exploiting a tragic situation, and I'm not going down that road without thinking the whole thing out.'

'Actually, I've been wondering about that myself,' Loveday replied thoughtfully. 'And I agree. We do have to be sensitive. But Laura was very positive that she wants the article to go ahead.' She glanced down at her watch. 'Actually, she wants to meet me again this afternoon. I said I'd give her a ring first.'

Merrick slumped back in his swivel chair with a loud sigh. 'Looks like she was right about this business not being a suicide. Just don't let her drag you into this. That's why we have the police.'

Loveday stared at him, narrowing her eyes. 'Who have you been talking to? Not that I need to ask . . .'

Merrick spread his hands, palms up to the ceiling. She looked away, controlling her annoyance. Sam had no right speaking to Merrick, even if he was one of his best mates. She was picturing the two of them standing at the bar of the Crab and Creel, pints of real ale on the counter in front of them, as they discussed her interfering ways. The trouble was, what Sam called *interfering in his cases*, Loveday considered *helping people*. If someone in trouble asked for her help, there was no way she would ever refuse. It was just that . . . well, sometimes the two seemed to cross over.

She looked up, annoyed that Merrick was still watching her. 'So what did Sam say?'

Merrick lifted his pen, rolling it between his fingers. He hesitated, choosing his words carefully. He'd no wish to kindle his young editor's fiery temper. He said, 'He understands you were only offering support to the widow, but . . . '

'I'll bet he said nothing of the kind. He asked you to tell me to back off . . . to stop poking my nose in.' She narrowed her eyes at him again. 'Be honest, Merrick. Isn't that what Sam said?'

Merrick gave a reluctant shrug. 'Not in so many words, but . . . '

Loveday released an exasperated sigh. 'Didn't you explain that it's my job to investigate things?'

Merrick stared at her. 'I did nothing of the kind. Since when did you become an investigative reporter, Loveday? That may be what you did when you worked on that Glasgow tabloid, but you're the editor of *Cornish Folk* now.' He shook his head, annoyed at his outburst. 'But it's got nothing to do with that.' He forced a smile into his voice. 'We just don't want you getting into another tight spot . . . not even for the best of reasons.'

'I'm sorry, Merrick. I just don't see how listening to Laura Venning's theory puts me in any danger.'

'I think you should have more faith in Sam. He didn't get to be a detective inspector by twiddling his thumbs and not listening to people. Leave the detecting to him, Loveday, the man knows what he's doing.'

Loveday glanced out to where Keri was making a show of typing into her computer, and smiled. She knew her colleague had been watching them, analyzing their body language, watching their expressions. If she'd been in the room with them, she'd have been agreeing with Merrick.

'OK,' Loveday sighed, getting up. 'Is that the lecture over?'

'That depends on whether you've paid any attention to it, or not.'

'All right, I promise not to get involved this time. OK?'

'Yeah, right!' Merrick muttered under his breath as he watched her go out the door.

Keri glanced up as Loveday came back into the office. 'Everything all right?'

'Have you got time for a coffee?'

Keri grinned, reaching for her bag. 'You've twisted my arm.'

The magazine occupied two floors of an elegant Georgian building in the centre of Truro. The street outside was quieter than normal. It was still mid-morning, too early for the lunchtime rush, but the office workers in Lemon Street would soon be emptying out onto the pavements and heading for the city's eateries. The two friends turned into the indoor market, and went upstairs to the gallery café where Loveday ordered two cappuccinos.

'Well?' Keri eyed her friend when they'd settled themselves at a table. 'Have you calmed down yet?'

Loveday sighed. 'Just about.'

'Care to tell me about it?'

'Would you believe Sam got Merrick to warn me off the Silas Venning murder?'

Keri's eyes flew open. 'I didn't know it was murder!'

'Well, it was. His widow said so all along, and I believed her.'

'So that was just the two of you thinking that, and not the police?' Keri had a mischievous twinkle in her eye.

Loveday ignored the remark. 'Sam's got the PM results, but he's not going public yet.'

Keri nodded. 'I suppose he has to be careful. The police need proof before they can go around accusing people of murder.'

Loveday stopped stirring her coffee and met Keri's eyes. '*I'm* not accusing anyone. How would I know who killed the man?'

'I'm guessing Sam thinks you might be considering finding out.'

'He would be wrong, then. Laura Venning has asked for my support, that's all. She's not expecting me to go snooping around.'

'Well, that's good to know.' Keri paused. 'So what was all the fuss about back there in Merrick's office?'

Loveday's blue eyes flashed. 'Sam went behind my back . . . to my boss. And that's just not acceptable.'

Keri was looking across at the café counter. She pushed back her chair. 'I'm having one of those donuts. Do you want one?'

Loveday shook her head. 'You'll get fat,

and Ben will leave you,' she called after her.

'Won't happen.' Keri smiled back over her shoulder before her eyes returned to the plate of sugary buns.

She returned, licking sticky fingers, and put the plate with its donut on the table. 'You were saying?'

But Loveday's initial annoyance had passed. She'd no intention of getting involved in somebody else's murder investigation . . . not this time. Her friends were right. She would leave this one to Sam.

If there was an elegant way to eat a donut, then Keri hadn't mastered it. Her mouth had a ring of sugary jam as she dabbed up the dropped crumbs. She said, 'Do we have to find another feature to fill the Laura Venning space?'

'Not sure yet. She's specifically asked that we still run the article, but Merrick and I are having second thoughts.'

Keri flicked the crumbs from her mouth. 'Running it would let us off the hook for finding a replacement piece, and if it's what she wants . . . '

Loveday pursed her lips, thinking. 'Maybe I'll find out more when I go back there this afternoon.'

'Wait a minute.' Keri put up a hand. 'I thought you said you would leave this one alone?'

'I said I wouldn't get involved in any snooping. I didn't say I wouldn't help her,' Loveday said.

'Help her to do what, exactly?' Keri was giving Loveday her *Are you mad?* look.

Loveday sighed. 'I'll know that when I get there, won't I?'

8

'We didn't catch your name,' Will said, after he had watched the huge man squeeze into the back of their car in the Venning Marine car park. He climbed in after him.

'Vance,' the man snarled.

'Vance who?' Will said. There was a pause when it seemed the man was considering if he needed to actually say more. 'It's not a hard question,' Will persisted. 'Just tell us your name.'

They waited. The man cleared his throat but the words still came out in a growl. 'Jesse Vance.'

Sam was watching the two of them in the driving mirror. Will adjusted his jacket. 'OK. What is this thing you wanted to tell us, Jesse?'

Vance's thumb flicked back to the boatyard. 'It's about them. They're trying to stitch Danny up, aren't they?'

Sam's and Will's eyes met in the driving mirror.

'He had nothing to do with it.'

'Nothing to do with what?' Will said.

Vance slid his eyes from one to the other. Had he just jumped in with both feet? He was trying to decide if this pair did actually know anything.

'Come on, Jesse. We haven't got all day. What is it that your pal Danny had nothing to do with?'

'It's nothing. I made a mistake.' Vance reached for the door handle to get out of the car, but Sam had flicked on the lock. He swivelled round to face Jesse.

'We're going nowhere till you cough up, Jesse. Or maybe you would like to accompany us to the station?'

Vance's dark beady eyes glared at Sam in the mirror. 'OK, so I got the wrong end of the stick. Right?' He was trying to stare Sam out, but Sam wasn't relenting. The man gave a heavy sigh that made his chins wobble. 'Look, I don't know nothing. Get it? How much plainer can that be?'

Sam changed tack. 'How long have you worked at Venning Marine, Jesse?'

The response was grudging. 'A year.'

'And what do you do here?'

Vance glanced back to the boatyard and frowned. 'I'm a gofer.'

Sam raised an eyebrow. 'A gofer?'

The big man glared at him again as if he was stupid. 'You know what a gofer is . . . I go for this, go for that. I'm at their bloody beck and call.'

Will glanced away to hide his amusement. He couldn't imagine anyone ordering this giant of a man around.

'I take it you don't like your employers,' Sam said.

'They're not my employers. I don't work there no more. I just came back for what's due me.' He glanced back at Venning Marine again. 'Bastards,' he muttered under his breath.

'Are we to understand that you didn't get your dues?' Will cut in. 'How much did they owe you?'

'A couple of grand,' Vance shot back before he could stop himself.

Will flashed Sam a surprised look, and received a nod in response, telling him to carry on with the line of questioning. He cleared his throat. 'A couple of grand sounds a lot of cash for a gofer. Think they would employ me?'

But Vance knew he'd already said too much. His fleshy lips were clamped tight together.

Will glanced back to the yard. 'What did you have to do to earn that much cash, Jesse?'

Vance ignored him. Will repeated the question. Vance continued to stare stubbornly across the car park.

Sam gave a heavy sigh. 'You know what? I've had enough of this.' He gunned up the engine, threw the car into gear, and they took off at a smart pace through the Venning Marine car park.

Vance swung round in alarm. 'What's he doing? Let me out of here!'

Will gave him a contented grin. 'Relax Jesse,' he said. 'Think of it as an invitation back to our place.'

9

Cassie had noticed the man hanging around the marina when she nipped out earlier to collect a cup of coffee and a sandwich. It was now late afternoon, and because of the dank, drabness of the day it was beginning to feel almost dark. The thought of walking past the man to the car park on her own filled her with trepidation. She couldn't be sure, but he looked a lot like the person who'd attacked Silas Venning that day. If it was him, then he had to be the same one she'd noticed working around the marina over the summer months.

Cassie was confused. Had this man put two and two together, and now realized that she was the one he had collided with at Venning Marine? Was he here now to get rid of her as a witness? She shivered.

She'd thought about ringing Sam, but what if her suspicions were wrong? She didn't want to look a fool in the eyes of her best friend's man. And she could hardly ring Adam for fear of panicking him. Loveday! That was it. She would ring Loveday. Calling in at Falmouth wouldn't be too much of a detour for her to make on the way home from Truro.

She punched in Loveday's name. The call was answered on the first ring.

'Cassie! Everything OK? I don't usually get the honour of a call from you at this time of day.'

'Yes, of course. Everything's fine.' Cassie swallowed. 'It's just that . . . well, I need your opinion on something, and I don't quite trust my own judgment.'

Loveday saved her work on the computer and stretched, easing out the stiffness in her back. Laura Venning had left a message cancelling the previously arranged appointment, but offering no reason. And although Loveday was curious about the woman's actions, it gave her the much-needed chance to type up her notes and write a new feature.

She frowned at the phone. 'You *are* aware that I know next to nothing about boats, Cassie?'

'It's not about boats . . . ' her friend hissed sharply, trying to control the shiver that was racing through her body.

Even over the phone, Loveday could pick up on her friend's distress. She was worried now. 'What's up, Cassie? What's wrong?'

Cassie fought back the growing unease as she moved along the deck of the *White Lady*, mobile phone in hand. Although everyone else had gone home for the day and she was alone, she took comfort from the fact the Loveday was at the other end of the line. 'Hang on a minute,' she said, wondering why she was whispering. She stretched forward, craning her neck to see if the dark shape of the man was still at the end of the boardwalk. It was.

'I'm in Falmouth . . . at the marina . . . on the *White Dancer*,' she whispered into the phone. 'It's the second-last boat on the boardwalk. Can you come down?'

'But are you OK?' Loveday repeated.

'Yes, I'm OK,' Cassie said. She sounded breathless. 'Just don't be long.'

'I'm on my way,' Loveday said, grabbing her bag and jacket.

The traffic was light as she sped along the A39, and twenty minutes later she was in Falmouth, speeding down the hill towards the marina. She spotted Cassie's big Land Rover immediately and pulled into the empty space beside it. A dishevelled-looking young man who was hanging about the security gate avoided Loveday's curious glance as she hurried past. She still had Cassie's security code from a previous visit, and punched it in, standing back as the gate swung open.

Loveday made her way along the boardwalk, quickening her step when she saw the *White Dancer*'s cabin lights. She stepped on board and tapped the door.

'It's me, Cassie. It's Loveday.'

The door opened slowly and Cassie's head came out. She gave Loveday a relieved grin and beckoned her inside.

Loveday followed her back down the steps into the cabin and then stood, hands on hips. 'Well, I'm here. Are you going to tell me now what's going on?'

Cassie grabbed her friend's wrist and pulled her over to the cabin window, jabbing a finger into the growing darkness.

'It's him. He's waiting to mug me, Loveday.' Her voice cracked. 'And I don't know what to do.'

Loveday peered out. The scruffy young man she'd noticed before was still there. She frowned. 'Who is he?'

'He's the one I was telling you about,' Cassie hissed. 'The one that attacked Silas Venning that day.'

Loveday reached for her phone, but Cassie grabbed it from her hand.

'What are you doing?'

Loveday couldn't stop her voice from rising. 'You have to tell the police about this, Cassie. I'm ringing Sam.'

'No!' Cassie looked horrified. 'What if there's a whole gang of them and they get to Adam and the kids? I'm not putting them in danger.'

Loveday took Cassie's hands and led her to the black leather bench seat. 'I very much doubt if he's one of a gang,' she said gently. 'It's only him out there. There's no one else hiding in the shadows.'

Cassie gave an unsure frown.

'Have you thought that he might not

even be waiting for you?'

'Of course he's waiting for me. Why else would he be there?'

Loveday picked up Cassie's denim jacket and handed it to her. 'There's only one way to find out.'

'What are you going to do?' Cassie's eyes were wide with alarm.

'We're going to ask him what he's doing there,' Loveday said firmly.

'I'm not sure about . . . '

'Have you got a better idea?' Loveday said. 'I mean, better than just staying locked up in this cabin.'

'What if he's armed?'

Loveday rolled her eyes. 'I didn't see a gun . . . come on.' She bundled Cassie up the stairs ahead of her, and off the yacht.

The man hadn't looked all that threatening to Loveday, but she was aware of Cassie shivering as they got closer to him. Both of them stopped as he called out.

'Mrs Trevillick? Are you Cassie Trevillick?'

Cassie squared her shoulders. 'What do you want?' she shouted back, trying to keep the tremor out of her voice.

'Can we talk?' the man asked as they

approached. He nodded back to the still-open café. 'My mum will make us a cup of tea.'

The two women stared at him.

'Your mum?' Cassie said, remembering the friendly woman behind the counter. 'That's your mum?'

The man nodded. 'And I'm Danny Santos. Look, I know you must be rushing to get home to your family, but this will just take a minute.'

Loveday looked away to hide an amused grin. Was this the young desperado who had so frightened Cassie? He looked about eighteen, with a flop of blond hair that almost obscured his eyes.

He held out an arm, leading the way. 'Your friend can come too,' he said.

10

Loveday was still smiling as she followed Cassie's 4 × 4 back to Marazion.

'You're going to tell Sam about this, aren't you?' Cassie said, when they had turned into the drive and she had climbed down from the Land Rover.

'You know I have to, Cassie. What Danny told us could be an important piece of evidence.'

'Well, you don't have to tell him everything, do you?'

Loveday grinned. 'You mean about you ringing me in a panic, and then hiding in the cabin of the boat until I got there, when all the lad wanted was to have a cup of tea and tell you his story?'

Cassie narrowed her eyes and flashed Loveday a warning look. 'Yes, that's the bit I don't want repeating.'

Loveday gave her a teasing grin as she linked arms with Cassie and walked with her to the back door of the big house. She patted her hand. 'Your secret's safe with me. Mind you, it will cost you a bottle of Chardonnay.'

'Does Sam know what a rogue his girlfriend is?' Cassie said, grinning back.

'Probably,' Loveday said with a wave as she disappeared into her cottage.

The cosy warmth of the kitchen was a welcome homecoming. She dumped her bag on the table and shrugged off her fleece-lined jacket, hanging it on the peg at the back of the door before going through to her tiny sitting room, flicking on lights as she went. She glanced at the remains of the charred logs in the fireplace, wishing she had set it as she normally did before leaving for work that morning.

Her phone buzzed, alerting her to the arrival of a new text. She went through to the kitchen and fished through her bag for it. It was from Sam, telling her he would be late arriving that evening. Loveday stared thoughtfully at the words, picturing him hurriedly punching out the message. He spent most nights at the cottage now, and yet she still didn't feel there was a permanency to the relationship.

They had never actually talked about it, but she knew he wasn't ready yet to give up his cottage in Stithian. It was the home he had shared with Tessa. The killing of Brian Penrose had brought it all to the surface. A wave of resentment swept over her. Sam never spoke about Tessa, but it was hard to accept she was still such a big part of his life. If the woman had still been a living, breathing person, she could at least have had something to compete with. How do you compete with a ghost?

Loveday tried to avoid picturing Sam and Tessa's first meeting, but it haunted her. He had mentioned they met in a pub in St Ives. It was one night when he and Will had called in for a beer; they'd been in the area to interview someone in connection with a case they had been working on the time.

Loveday could picture Tessa in the middle of a group of her artist friends, laughing, her glorious chestnut-coloured hair tumbling over her shoulders. She could imagine her looking up and meeting Sam's admiring eyes, and then smiling. It was an image that still tortured Loveday. She had no idea how that scene had really played out. Sam had never gone into any detail, but it had been the start of their love affair and the subsequent marriage.

Loveday put the phone down with a sigh and went through to set the fire in the sitting room. An hour later, there was a cheerful blaze in the hearth, and she'd taken a shower before dressing in a long floral skirt with a blouse in shades of autumn. Two thick steaks were waiting to be set under the grill, and there was a salad in the fridge.

She opened a bottle of chilled white wine and poured a glass for herself, taking it through to the fire. She was on her second glass when she heard Sam's car in the drive and went to meet him. The weather had changed since she and Cassie had got back, and rain glistened on the windscreen of the car. Sam looked tired, but the pleasure in his eyes when he saw her in the doorway made Loveday's heart flip over. She stretched up to kiss him before leading him into the warm cottage.

Sam leaned against the doorjamb, watching Loveday move around the kitchen as she prepared their meal. It felt good, being here with her. It felt like home. He thought of his cold, empty cottage back in Stithian. There was no welcome there, and yet he'd held onto it. Loveday had never suggested he should do otherwise, and he wondered, not for the first time, how strong their relationship was. And yet it felt right. Now, seeing her as glowing and beautiful as she was tonight, he thought himself a very contented, lucky man.

Loveday waited until they had eaten and had dealt with the dishes, and were settled in front of the fire, before she began to relate what had happened earlier.

Sam put his glass of malt whisky on the table beside the sofa and frowned at her. 'You mean this guy was lurking around the marina watching Cassie, and she rang you instead of me?' His voice was incredulous. 'What on earth did she think you could do? You should have contacted me, Loveday.'

'Cassie begged me not to. She said she didn't want any fuss.'

Sam was shaking his head. 'And what if this bloke had attacked her . . . attacked both of you?'

Loveday put up a hand. 'I know what you're saying, Sam, but you weren't there; and as it turned out, everything was fine.'

'Carry on,' Sam said stiffly.

Loveday could tell he was angry. She took a breath. 'I saw the guy the minute I reached the marina security gate. Cassie had given me the code, and I could see him watching me as I punched in the numbers. Cassie was waiting for me on the *White Dancer*.' She glanced across to him. 'She was really scared, Sam. This guy had really freaked her out. She recognized him as the one who attacked Silas Venning that day.'

Sam bit back his anger. He couldn't believe Loveday hadn't called him. He sat back, still fuming, as she took up her story again.

'We obviously couldn't stay on board the boat all night, so I convinced Cassie that we had to get out of there.' She paused for a breath. 'The guy stepped forward as we approached the security gate. He called Cassie by name.'

She took a sip of her wine and cradled the glass in her hands. 'It turned out that his mother runs the little café just outside the marina.'

Sam nodded. 'We were there today.'

'Were you? Cassie didn't say.' Loveday glanced briefly at him and then continued. 'Apparently, he sometimes used to work at Venning Marine; Silas sacked him, but that wasn't the reason for his anger.' She bit her lip. She wasn't looking forward to telling him the next bit. 'He had this mate in prison.' She slid him a glance, not sure how to go on. 'It was Brian Penrose.'

Sam said nothing.

'Best mates, according to him,' Loveday continued. 'Anyway, he said Venning was attempting to intimidate Penrose inside jail. It was getting close to Penrose's release date, and he'd been threatening to go to

160

the police with certain information about Venning Marine. Our new acquaintance said he'd tried to talk him out of it, reminding him how nasty Silas Venning could be, but Penrose apparently refused to be persuaded, and made no secret of his intentions.'

She broke off, meeting Sam's eyes. 'Did you know that Penrose had been beaten up while he was inside? Quite badly, by all accounts. It was because of that — '

'Stop!' Sam's hand went up. 'Your informant wouldn't be Danny Santos, by any chance?'

Loveday stared at him. 'You know him?'

'We do, but Amanda Fox hasn't been able to track him down so far.'

'That would be because he's been lying low,' Loveday said.

'Never mind about that now. We'll winkle him out tomorrow. Just tell me what he said about his assault on Venning.'

Loveday took another sip of her wine. 'Danny visited Penrose in prison and was shocked when he saw his injuries. As I said, he'd been really badly beaten,

161

apparently. According to Danny, his attacker had all but killed him.

'Danny was in no doubt at all that Venning had ordered this attack. He just saw red and went after Venning.'

She ran a finger around the rim of her glass. 'Poor Danny,' she said quietly. 'If only he'd thought about it, he probably wouldn't have been so rash. After all, if Venning was capable of doing that to Penrose while he was inside, what might he do to Danny?'

'And you believed all of this?' Sam asked.

Loveday's shoulders lifted in a shrug. 'No reason not to. If you had seen how scared he was, you would have believed him too. I know it stretches credulity, but according to Danny, Silas was heavily into drugs — smuggling, I mean.' She shifted into a more comfortable position on the sofa. 'I'm not saying it was any big-scale operation, but the story goes that drugs definitely changed hands when new Venning Marine yachts went off on their sea trials.

'As Danny tells it, the packets of drugs

were collected off the coast, and left on board the new vessels when they returned to their moorings at the boatyard. People posing as potential buyers picked them up later.'

Sam's eyes slid up to the ceiling, and Loveday said, 'OK, I know it all sounds a bit far-fetched, but apparently Silas depended on the extra bit of income to keep his business operational.'

Despite how unlikely it all sounded, the story did tie it in with what Liam Barnes had told them about Venning Marine being in trouble. It set Sam wondering about the other boatyard in Penzance — the one that was allegedly stealing all of Venning's business. Could they also be involved in drugs?

11

Loveday couldn't get Silas Venning out of her mind next day as she drove to Truro. None of them knew Danny Santos, but why should he lie? If Penrose really had been beaten up in prison, it would be easy enough for Sam to check; but, even so, it wouldn't confirm that Silas had anything to do with it.

Reading Sam's mind the previous night had not been difficult. He would be thinking that Santos could be in the frame for Silas's murder. But, wait — that couldn't be right either, she realized, because Silas had already been dead before Penrose had even been released.

She shook her head, sighing. The traffic up front had come to a near-standstill as it approached the main roundabout into Truro. Loveday muttered a curse. It would be a crawl into town from here on in. She made a mental note to follow Sam's lead in future, and set off for the office before Cornwall's morning traffic got going.

It was twenty minutes later when she eventually turned into the magazine's car park, and she still hadn't reached a conclusion about who killed Silas. The clock on the dashboard told her it was ten past nine. Loveday's thoughts went to the CID suite at the police station across town. She tried to picture Sam at the morning briefing with his team. He'd called in the previous night, leaving a message instructing DC Amanda Fox to bring Danny Santos in for questioning.

Loveday had no idea how she would find Danny. He'd refused to give her and Cassie his address. Maybe they could track him down through his mother?

It crossed her mind that perhaps Laura Venning had known all along what her husband had been up to. If Venning Marine was in financial trouble, then she must surely have been aware of it. She toyed with the idea of paying the woman another visit, but a little voice in her head was telling her to stay out of it. Two people had been murdered. This was serious, and she really didn't fancy being the killer's next victim.

Her mobile phone rang as she was running up the stairs to the editorial office. It was Cassie.

'I tried to catch you before you drove off this morning. Did you tell Sam about Santos?'

'Yes, I did.'

'And?'

Loveday tut-tutted. 'You know I can't tell you.'

'But he is going to investigate it?' Cassie sounded worried.

'I'm sure Sam will do what he has to, but he doesn't share the details of his investigations with me.' She stopped, frowning, as she reached the door into the editorial suite. 'Is something wrong, Cassie?' Loveday could hear the sound of traffic at the other end of the phone, and knew Cassie must be on her way to the Falmouth Marina.

'No, it's all good,' Cassie said, but she sounded distracted. 'I just have to sort out a couple of last-minute snag things, and then the White Dancer will be ready to hand back to her owners.' She paused. 'I don't suppose you could be free for lunch?'

'Yes, why not? Just name the place and I'll be there.'

Keri lowered her head in a conspiratorial whisper as Loveday walked into the room. 'Merrick's been asking for you. And he's on the warpath.'

Loveday glanced across to Merrick's office. Keri was right. He didn't look happy. He was beckoning her in. She frowned, slipping off her red wool coat. 'Why is he on the warpath?'

Keri shrugged. 'Search me.'

'Close the door and take a seat,' Merrick said as Loveday entered his office. She sat down, curious to know what was coming.

'I had a call from Laura Venning last evening.'

She waited for him to go on. He was studying her, trying to assess if she knew what he was about to say. She gave him a vacant expression.

He cleared his throat. 'She says you took something from her home.'

Loveday blinked. 'She said what? I don't understand. Is she accusing me of stealing from her?' She could feel her anger rising.

Merrick leaned back and the old revolving chair gave its familiar creak. Loveday could tell by his face that he wasn't enjoying this any more than she was.

He continued, 'She says you took a valuable necklace.'

'What?!'

Merrick had hardly needed to ask if the accusation was true. The look of astonishment on Loveday's face told him all he needed to know. He hadn't believed the woman's story for a moment, but he'd been duty-bound to follow it through. 'Look, I know you didn't do this, Loveday, but Laura Venning is a dangerous woman and we have to tread carefully. Have you any idea why she would make such an accusation?'

The colour had drained from Loveday's face. 'Absolutely none.' She was stunned.

'The thing is,' Merrick went on, 'she says she is prepared to overlook the thing if you agree to return the necklace to

168

Trevore. She wants to see you this morning.'

'But I haven't got her stupid necklace.' She started to get up. 'I need to tell Sam about this.'

'No. Wait!' Merrick waved her back into her chair. 'Think about it first, Loveday. What reason could this woman have for accusing you?'

Loveday shrugged. 'I have absolutely no idea.'

Merrick glanced out to Loveday's desk, and the big leather shoulder bag she carried that contained all her working paraphernalia. 'Do you empty that every night?'

'Well, no. Only if I have notes to type up, and then I'll take out my notebook and digital recorder.'

'Would you like to bring it in here and empty it out now?'

Loveday flashed him a look of outrage. 'You surely don't believe this woman, do you?'

'Of course I don't,' Merrick said. 'But if Laura Venning is to make an accusation like this stick, then she will have planted the evidence.'

Loveday followed his glance back to her bag, and her eyes went wide with disbelief. 'You think that necklace is in my bag?'

Merrick spread his hands. 'Let's just say the lovely Laura is not to be trusted.'

Loveday got up, striding out of Merrick's office to her desk. She seized the shoulder bag and, ignoring Keri's puzzled look, marched back to her boss. She uncoupled the catch of the bag and tipped the contents onto Merrick's desk — notebook, recorder, collection of pens, car keys, hairbrush, make-up bag, a couple of scrunched-up tissues . . . Loveday started. It looked like something had been wrapped in one of the tissues. Her fingers shook as she opened it, revealing a pearl necklace with a diamond clip.

She stared in disbelief, sinking back onto the chair. 'I really do need to speak to Sam now,' she said, her voice shaking with rage.

'Well, you'd better take the necklace with you,' Merrick said, sliding open a drawer in his desk and fishing out a roll of small plastic bags. 'I knew these would come in useful if I kept them long enough.' He grinned at her.

Loveday lifted the necklace, still in its tissue wrap, and placed it in the plastic bag, being careful not to touch it.

'Let me know what Sam says,' Merrick called after her as she left his office.

Sam answered his phone on the third ring. 'Loveday! Look, can I call you back? I'm a bit — '

'I need to speak to you, Sam. Like, now!'

He began to protest, but she stopped him. 'It's really important. Can I come over?'

'Is something wrong, Loveday?' An edge of concern had jumped into his voice.

'I'll tell you when I see you. I'm on my way now.'

It took Loveday ten minutes to hurry through the city streets to the police station. She felt like a nervous child as she waited for him to come down to the front counter.

Sam looked slightly flustered when he arrived, and Loveday guessed he wasn't comfortable with her being here in his domain. He touched her arm. 'You'd better come up to my office.'

When they had reached the privacy of the lift, he put his arms around her. 'What's wrong, Loveday?' His voice was full of concern.

Loveday tapped the shoulder bag. 'It's in here. You have to see this for yourself.'

When they reached his office, Loveday closed the door and reached into her bag for the necklace. Sam narrowed his eyes and stared at it on his desk. Sunlight streaming in from the window was catching the diamond clasp, and it glinted through the plastic bag.

'You haven't touched this, I hope,' he said, looking up at Loveday.

She shook her head.

'And you've never seen it before today?'

'Of course I haven't,' she snapped. 'It was planted on me . . . *she* planted it on me.'

Sam moved to the door and called in DS Will Tregellis, who gave Loveday a smile as he entered the room.

Sam indicated the necklace. 'Can you get one of the fingerprint boys to go over this, Will?' He looked at Loveday. 'We'll have to take your prints, I'm afraid, Loveday. It's the only way we can prove that you never touched this.'

Loveday nodded. 'I understand.'

'Can I trust you not to do anything further about this? And certainly don't speak to Laura Venning again until I get back to you.'

'You have my word,' Loveday assured him as she turned to follow Will from the room. She looked back as she reached the door. 'Thank you, Sam.'

12

'It was the closest place I could find to your office,' Cassie said as Loveday pulled out a chair and sat down opposite her friend in the pizza restaurant. 'Is it OK?'

'It's fine,' Loveday said with a sigh. Lunch was the last thing on her mind. The more she thought about that necklace, the angrier she got. It was hurtful to be accused of stealing, no matter how ridiculous it was. For heaven's sake, she had been nice to the woman, had even offered to help her. Why would she turn on her like this?

'Oh dear,' Cassie said, giving Loveday an anxious look across the table. 'You don't look in a good place today. Tell Auntie Cassie.'

Loveday shook her head. 'It's nothing,' But it wasn't nothing. She hadn't done anything wrong. It was Laura Venning who should be ashamed of her behaviour.

'She did what?' Cassie's voice rose in astonishment when Loveday had recounted the morning's events. 'But why? I mean, why would she do a thing like that?'

'I've absolutely no idea,' Loveday said.

A young, sullen-faced waitress appeared at their table, notepad in hand.

'Could you give us a few minutes?' Cassie smiled up at her. 'We're not quite ready to order yet.'

The girl gave a disinterested shrug and wandered off to one of the other tables.

Cassie turned back to Loveday. 'She must have had a reason. You didn't upset her, did you?'

Loveday laughed. 'Thanks for the vote of confidence. I don't make a habit of going around upsetting people.'

'No, of course you don't. What does Sam say?'

'He's told me to wait until the fingerprint results are in, and then it's pretty much up to me what I do after that.' But Loveday had already decided. She was due an explanation. She would confront the Venning woman — and sooner rather than later. But she was curious too. 'How well do you know her, Cassie?'

'Hardly at all,' Cassie said. 'I didn't even know Silas all that well. Venning Marine was a top boatyard that attracted customers from the big-money bracket.' She slid Loveday a mischievous grin. 'My kind of people.'

'Potential customers for your business, you mean,' Loveday said.

Cassie nodded. 'I approached the company with a few suggestions about what my company could do for his business, and Silas suggested we should discuss my proposal over lunch. He was charming. He put a lot of business my way.'

The glum-faced waitress was back, and the friends made quick choices from the menu. The girl scribbled down their orders and moved away.

'Venning Marine also has a fairly robust business buying and selling secondhand yachts, which was where I came in. Many of them needed a complete refurb, and a good chunk of that business was passed on to me.'

Loveday was fiddling with her cutlery, absent-mindedly rearranging the knife and fork. 'What about Laura? How often did you meet her?'

'At press launches, mostly. When the yard brought out a new vessel they always made a big song and dance about it, especially if a celebrity buyer was involved. Laura was a very charismatic hostess, but protective of Silas at all times.'

'Was it at one of these dos that you met Meredith Deering?'

Cassie nodded. 'I liked Meredith. Laura introduced her to me as her best friend. I think they grew up together. I got the impression that she and Silas regarded her as part of the family.'

Loveday chewed on a piece of pizza, and sighed. 'I think she can say goodbye to that now. She lied to Laura about Silas's health, and needless to say, the lady herself didn't exactly appreciate it.'

'Well, that figures.' Cassie sliced off a piece of pizza and put it into her mouth. 'As I said, Laura was very protective of her husband. She always seemed to have her eye on him, to the extent of appearing instantly at his side if she saw a predatory female homing in.'

Loveday raised an eyebrow. 'Did that happen often?'

'What? Predatory females circling?' Cassie laughed. 'The other way round, I think. You must have heard of his reputation, Loveday. Silas loved the ladies. He even tried it on with me a couple of times; but when he realized that was going nowhere, he left me alone.'

'I wonder how Laura coped with that,' Loveday said thoughtfully. The friends continued their conversation between mouthfuls of pizza.

'If anything,' Cassie stated, 'you must know Laura Venning better than me. You've interviewed her.'

Loveday's mind went back that interview in Laura's studio. It had been a strange meeting, and she remembered leaving her that day feeling she knew no more about the woman than when she'd arrived. Laura Venning was a person in total control of herself, a complex individual. Loveday could not imagine the woman doing anything without a reason, which made the planting of a necklace on her all the more sinister.

She used her fork to push the uneaten half of her pizza to the side of the plate. 'I take it you never suspected Silas was involved in drug smuggling?'

Cassie's head jerked up. 'Definitely not. I still don't believe it. And as for killing anyone . . . ' Her words trailed off. 'The man wasn't a saint, but he wasn't into that kind of stuff.'

Loveday suddenly remembered it was Cassie who had suggested they meet up for lunch. 'I'm sorry, Cassie. Was there something you wanted to talk to me about?'

'We're doing it,' Cassie said. 'I just needed to get this whole Venning Marine business out of my head.'

'You'll have lost a lot of business now,' Loveday said.

Cassie shrugged. 'A bit, but I never put all my eggs in one basket. Anyway, I have my eye on another contract with a boatyard in Penzance that could turn out to be quite lucrative.'

13

Loveday was back in the office when Sam called.

'You're in the clear,' he said. 'Only two sets of prints on that necklace, and neither of them yours.'

Loveday bristled. 'What d'you mean, *in the clear*? Of course I am. I never saw that necklace before.'

'Whoa . . . don't get crinkly. It was a joke.'

She could hear the amusement in his voice. 'Sorry, Sam. I'm just a bit strung out today. You said two sets of fingerprints?'

'That's right. Presumably one of them will be Mrs Venning's, and I'm assuming the others will belong to Silas. We'll be cross-checking that with the body.'

Loveday nodded into the phone. 'So, what happens now? Do I take the necklace back to her, and ram it down her throat?'

'No, we'll do that — return it, I mean, not ram it down her throat. You should stay out of it from now on, Loveday. I've no idea why Laura Venning did what she did, but it's in our court now and we'll deal with it.'

'That's all very well for you to say, Sam, but it was my good name she tried to besmirch.' She paused and gave an indignant cluck. 'Nobody has ever accused me of stealing before. It's not pleasant.'

'I know,' Sam said, 'and I can understand your anger. But this is a murder case now, and this woman is the victim's widow. You have to step back from it.' He waited, and when Loveday didn't respond, he added, 'You do understand that, Loveday, don't you?'

She understood all right, but there was no way she would leave this alone . . . not until she knew what was going on. She swallowed hard. 'OK, Sam. I hear what you're saying.'

Sam stared at the phone after Loveday had clicked off the call. She might have heard his warning, but there was no guarantee she would heed it.

He was remembering the first time he saw her. Loveday had been working with an artist friend, Lawrence Kemp, doing a photoshoot for the magazine on the cliffs out at Borlase, when they found a body down in one of the coves. The investigation had turned up a potentially incriminating link between Kemp and the dead man, making him their main suspect. Sam gave a grim smile, recalling how Loveday had gone into crusading mode to defend Kemp to such an extent as to put herself in danger. At the time, he had been more annoyed at her interference than anything else. This time, she meant so much more to him. He had already lost one woman he loved; he didn't want to lose another. He would reinforce his warning to her at the cottage later. He could only hope she would listen.

Merrick was typing furiously into his computer when Loveday glanced across at his office. Keri followed her gaze. 'He's doing his blog post,' she said with a giggle. 'And you know how much he enjoys that.'

The magazine already had a popular

Cornish Folk website that got hits from all over the world. The additional blog had been Loveday's idea. She would have been happy to set it up, but Merrick decided he should be the one to front it. It wasn't a task he relished, but his wry sense of humour and tales of everyday life as the publisher of the popular magazine had a following. Each of his weekly blog posts attracted an impressive string of comments. Loveday wasn't complaining.

She crossed the floor to his room and knocked briefly. Merrick looked up and waved her in. He sat back from his computer keyboard, extracted the pencil he had tucked behind his ear and raised an enquiring eyebrow. 'Please tell me this is good news.'

Loveday put up a hand, laughing. 'It is. At least, I think it is. Sam's fingerprint people checked out the necklace — and guess what?' She didn't wait for a response. 'My fingerprints *weren't* on it,' she said triumphantly.

Merrick shook his head. 'That woman is a mystery. She must have known you could prove you had nothing to do with her precious necklace.'

'Well, no, not really, Merrick. It would have been the most natural thing in the world for me to have handled it after I'd found it. She would have been depending on me being that naïve.'

Merrick nodded. 'What's Sam saying about it?'

Loveday scowled. 'What do you think? He's told me to forget it.'

'And will you?'

'Will I do what I'm told?' She was on her way to the door as she turned and grinned back at him. 'What do you think?'

The initial surge of outrage and indignation Loveday had felt when Merrick told her about Laura Venning's ridiculous accusation had long since left her, but she was curious now as to what the woman had to gain by doing something like this. On the drive to Trevore, she practised what she would say when she saw Laura. If it was the last thing she did, she would get an explanation for the woman's behaviour. She hadn't rung ahead. She wasn't making any appointments. She would confront the woman head on.

There were no vehicles in the drive, but that didn't necessarily mean no one was at home. Loveday knew there was a big double garage at the side of the house, and Laura's car could very well be in there. She rang the bell, and kept her finger on it until someone answered the door. It was the same grey-haired, middle-aged woman Loveday had met on her first visit — and she didn't look pleased to see her.

'Is she in?' Loveday wasn't standing on ceremony.

'Mrs Venning is not seeing anyone today,' the maid said stiffly, as though Loveday was an unwelcome double-glazing salesperson.

'She'll see me,' Loveday said, sweeping past the woman.

Laura Venning was in her elegant sitting room, standing by the fire, a glass of red wine in her hand. She was dressed in a white catsuit, with a black scarf knotted at her throat. Loveday had only ever seen similar outfits in sixties films.

The woman smiled. 'Loveday! What a surprise. Do come in.'

The grey-haired woman had followed her into the room, but Laura waved her out, and she left with a shake of her head.

'Why did you try to set me up, Mrs Venning?' Loveday was fighting to keep her voice steady. 'I think I'm owed an explanation.'

Laura smiled. 'Can I offer you a drink?'

'I haven't come for a drink. I think you should know that the police have your necklace now, Mrs Venning. I took it to them. They ran a fingerprint check on it, and guess what? My prints were not on it.'

'No, they wouldn't be, would they? Not when you have so many friends in the force.'

Loveday threw her head back and stared at the ceiling. 'Are you suggesting the police are in on this now?' she said in exasperation.

'Sit down, Loveday. I'm teasing you. I made a mistake and I apologize. I shouldn't have put the necklace in your bag, and I shouldn't have rung your publisher. It was silly of me.' She took a sip of her wine and put the glass on the white mantelpiece. 'But if I hadn't, you wouldn't be here now.' She came forward and took Loveday's hands in hers. 'And I really need your help.'

Loveday pulled her hands free and stared at the woman. 'You rang my boss and accused me of stealing! How could you do a thing like that?'

Laura shrugged. 'I'm sorry. I hope you can forgive me. I was desperate, and this was the only way I could think to secure your involvement.'

'My *involvement*?' What was the woman talking about?

Laura moved around the sofa and sat down, smiling up at Loveday. 'In solving my husband's murder, of course.'

Loveday stepped back and sank slowly onto the sofa opposite. She was trying to work out if the woman was completely mad, or just a very misguided grieving widow. The police were handling this now. Wasn't that what she wanted?

Laura put her hands together. 'I can see that you're confused. Let me explain. The police came to see me and told me they were now treating Silas's death as murder, just as I have been trying to convince everyone all along . . . but they think Meredith did it.'

She gave an incredulous laugh. 'I mean . . . Meredith? How could they even consider that? She is one of the meekest people I know. She saves lives, for God's sake, she doesn't extinguish them.'

Loveday put her fingers to her temples as though some understanding might pour from them into her brain. 'Just let me get this right. You want *me* to solve your husband's murder?'

The woman nodded. 'I'll help you, of course; but yes, that's about the size of it.'

'And how exactly do you suggest I do that?'

Laura got up and moved round behind the sofa to retrieve her wine glass. She drained it and then headed for the drinks tray for a refill. 'I know the background to all this,' she said. 'I could point you in the right direction.'

Loveday frowned. 'So why can't you point the police in the right direction?'

'Because they won't listen to me. They'd think I'm just a sad, demented woman.' She threw Loveday a knowing glance. 'But I know what I know, and I need your help to prove it.'

Loveday released a long sigh. 'Sit down, please, Mrs Venning.' She waited until the woman had complied. 'Now, just tell me what it is that you think you know.'

Laura Venning threw back the wine she was holding and fiddled with the stem of the glass. Her voice had a slight slur. 'Silas was attacked in his office a few weeks ago . . . '

'Yes, by Danny Santos. I know about that.'

Laura's eyes flew open. 'You know about it?'

Loveday nodded. 'And so do the police. Is this your new evidence?'

The woman ran the tip of her tongue over her lips to moisten them. Loveday could almost see the wheels in her head whirring. 'But they don't know about Liam Barnes. He's taken over from Silas, at Venning Marine. At least, that's what he thinks, and it suits me to leave him with that assumption for now.'

She leaned forward. 'He has been working behind the scenes to undermine Silas for years, but recently things got worse. He thinks I don't know, but he's in cahoots with Clayton-Barratt, our main rivals. They have a boatyard in Penzance.

'They know what we're doing almost before we even know ourselves, and there's only one way that is possible.' She stopped, glancing across at Loveday for dramatic impact. 'Someone is feeding them information. I suspect they are even getting copies of our new designs.'

'Hang on a minute,' Loveday said. 'You're suggesting that some kind of commercial espionage is going on, and that this Mr Barnes is behind it?'

'He's the only one who has this kind of information.'

'I didn't realize you were so involved in the business, Mrs Venning. In fact, you led me to believe you took no interest in it.'

'It's my money in that business, Miss Ross. I might not take an active part in the day-to-day running of it, but you can be assured that I make it my business to know everything that's going on.'

It was the first believable thing the woman had said. If she knew so much about what was going on, then she must her aware of her late husband's dalliance with drugs running. She never mentioned that.

Laura Venning was watching her. 'Well? Are you on board or not?' she said.

Loveday glanced away, hoping the woman would assume she was considering it. But there was no way she would work undercover for Laura Venning, and she certainly had no intention of going behind Sam's back. He would be very interested to hear about this tonight.

'I'll have to think about it,' she said, getting up. 'Is this everything, or do you have any other little surprises to spring?'

Laura stood up with her. 'Liam is coming over this evening with the company books.' She gave Loveday a dazzling smile. 'So I might well have more information for you in the morning.'

On the short drive back to Truro, Loveday tried to assemble her thoughts. She didn't know what she'd been expecting from Laura Venning, but it wasn't this.

She couldn't make the woman out at all. But one thing was certain: she was not doing very much grieving for her dead husband.

★ ★ ★

Loveday was mentally scolding herself as she ran up the stairs to her office. She was the editor of *Cornish Folk*, and she hadn't done a stroke of work all day. There had been a string of calls in her absence. Keri had jotted them all down, and now Loveday tried to settle at her desk to deal with them. She had scheduled in two main pieces of writing, and she had two choices. Either she could stay late — very late — or she could download the transcripts at home and work on them there. The decision was made easier when Sam rang, explaining he would be working late that evening, and would just stay over at his cottage in Stithian.

'You don't mind, do you, Loveday? It just makes more sense to stay there tonight.'

She did actually mind, but she had no

intention of letting Sam know that. The last thing she wanted was to appear possessive. They had made no definite commitment to each other. He was perfectly at liberty to spend the night in his own cottage if that was what he wanted.

Loveday forced herself to smile. 'Actually, that probably suits me too. I've a load of work to do at home tonight.'

After the call, Sam tossed his mobile onto the desk and drew his eyebrows together. She could at least have sounded a little disappointed. But then she had work to do. Loveday didn't normally bring work home. Why couldn't she have finished it at the office? He chewed the inside of his cheek, thinking. And then he knew why. Loveday hadn't been in the office all afternoon. She had been at Laura Venning's house!

14

There was so much stuff whirling around Loveday's mind as she turned off the main road onto the hill that led down into Marazion that she was beginning to feel quite giddy. She'd gone over that scene with Laura Venning so many times already, and still she couldn't decide what the woman was playing at. She needed to talk it through with someone. The obvious person would be Sam, but she could already predict his reaction if he thought she was even considering meddling in his work.

She couldn't believe the woman she had left only hours ago was the same sophisticated, talented — if more than a bit arrogant — artist she had interviewed before all of this happened. What did she think Loveday could do that the police couldn't? The notion was ridiculous, and yet she was considering it.

As she drove down the steep, narrow

hill into the village, Loveday thought of knocking on Cassie's door when she parked up at the side of the cottage. But, at the last minute, she'd decided to stay on at the office to finish her work. It was almost nine o'clock now, and she knew Cassie and Adam would be relaxing after getting the children off to bed. She would have to let this simmer in her mind until she'd decided what was the best way forward.

It was another hour before Loveday realized she was hungry, but the fridge needed replenishing again. If Sam was here he would take her down to the Godolphin for a meal. She gave a wry smile. He never minded how disorganized she was on the domestic front. She found some crackers in the biscuit tin, and a chunk of cheddar in the fridge. Piling them onto a tray with a jar of sweet pickle, she took them back to the sitting room.

Loveday was halfway through her makeshift feast when she heard the car coming up the drive. Her heart gave a little lurch. Sam must have decided to come after all. She jumped up, running a hand over her smooth dark hair, and went to meet him.

But the person getting out of the smart red BMW wasn't Sam. The woman was in her sixties, smart and petite, with a confident, assured stride. Even in this light, Loveday could see the short, silver-grey hair was elegantly styled; and when the woman extended a hand to introduce herself, a gold bracelet jangled and the diamonds on her fingers sparkled.

'Forgive me for calling at such a late hour unannounced like this. I'm Geraldine Anstey,' she said. 'Laura's mother.'

Loveday's expression did not mask her surprise. She shook the hand that was offered and stood back for the woman to come into the cottage. She didn't accept the seat Loveday offered, but remained standing, glancing nervously around the room. Loveday had lit the fire and the place looked cosy, even if it was designed for comfort more than elegance. A picture of that beautiful room at Trevore flitted briefly into Loveday's mind. Her little cottage hardly came up to that standard

— but it was her home, and she was more than happy with it.

Geraldine Anstey gave a nervous cough. 'I'm sure you know why I am here.' She paused, glancing across to Loveday. 'I want to apologize for my daughter.' Her voice faltered and she took a steadying breath before continuing. 'Laura told me about the necklace . . . well, she didn't exactly tell me. I knew something was wrong and forced it out of her.' She glanced away, hoping Loveday wouldn't notice how she bit her lip. 'Look, I know you didn't try to steal the blessed necklace. I can't imagine why my daughter would want to make it appear as though you had. It was an appalling thing for Laura to do.'

Her bottom lip was quivering now, and Loveday could see the woman was struggling to hang onto her emotions. Loveday sprang forward and took Geraldine's arm, guiding her round to the sofa. She smiled down at her. 'I was just about to make a pot of tea. Would you like some?'

'No. Thank you. I won't be stopping. This wasn't intended to be a social call.'

She locked earnest grey eyes with Loveday's. 'I understand you have gone to the police?'

'Only to establish my innocence. I'm not planning to pursue it any further. What exactly did Laura tell you, Mrs Anstey?'

The woman had been holding herself rigid in an obvious desperate attempt to retain her dignity. But now she almost collapsed with relief. All pretence of anything else had disappeared. For a moment, Loveday thought the woman was about to burst into tears, and her first instinct was to reach out and hug her, but Geraldine was quickly regaining her composure.

'My daughter is not in a very good place at the moment, Miss Ross. She's taking her husband's death hard.'

Loveday's thoughts swung back to that scene in Laura Venning's house. Her actions might have been misguided, and not just a little wacky, but there had been no sign of grief, just a determination for the tragic situation to be resolved in the way she wanted.

'Laura and Silas were very close, you see,' Geraldine was continuing. 'She's just finding all this difficult to deal with.'

'Yes,' Loveday said thoughtfully. 'I'm sure she must be.' She glanced away, wishing she believed this. She was remembering those initials carved into the tree in Bolger's Wood. Had she misjudged Laura Venning?

She wondered if Laura had also shared with her mother her crazy idea to launch her own investigation into Silas's death. Could this visit be another attempt to get her on board with the crackpot scheme? She could always ask her, of course, but somehow she didn't feel that would be a good idea.

'Laura said you and your husband have just returned from a Caribbean cruise.'

Mrs Anstey shrugged. 'We cut it short, but that didn't matter. We just wanted to get home after Liam contacted us.' She smiled. 'He's been looking after Laura. He's been a brick, taking charge at Venning Marine in the way he did. He's the one who has kept it all going.'

Liam Barnes! Only hours earlier, Laura had told her she suspected the man of treachery. Now, according to her mother, he was Laura's salvation. Both versions couldn't be right. This was also the man Laura had told her was visiting her tonight to go over the company books. Or was that just a cover for a more personal relationship? She was confused.

The relief that her daughter was not to be prosecuted for falsely accusing Loveday of theft had loosened the woman's tongue. 'It was a blessing the day Liam joined the business, even if Silas didn't always appreciate him.'

Loveday's head jerked up. 'Didn't the two men get on, then?'

'What?' Geraldine Anstey coloured. She was talking too much. She had to watch what she was saying now. 'Yes, of course they got on. Liam was like Silas's right arm. It was just that . . . well, when people work so closely together there are sometimes differences.' She shrugged. 'It happens in all companies, even ours. Graham and I haven't always seen eye to eye, but we both recognize that people bring their own strengths to a business, and that is not a bad thing.'

Loveday remembered the couple ran

one of the county's most successful, not to mention profitable, property development businesses.

'Losing your son-in-law in such a tragic way must be awful for you, and your husband as well . . . with you being such a close family, I mean.' It was a shot in the dark, but Loveday was interested to see how Mrs Anstey would react to the suggestion that she and her husband liked Silas Venning.

Before the woman glanced away Loveday thought she caught a look of irritation in the fine grey eyes. But she quickly regained her composure. 'Of course we were. Dear Silas will be sadly missed.'

The phrase kept running through Loveday's mind long after Geraldine Anstey had left. It didn't sound convincing. Had the Ansteys thought their daughter had married beneath her? Did they resent Silas's philandering ways? And what about Dr Meredith Deering? Wasn't she supposed to be Laura's best friend — the friend she'd grown up with? Geraldine had never even mentioned her.

The woman's entire visit had unsettled Loveday, for it raised more questions than it had answered. She was in no doubt that there had been no love lost between Laura and Silas.

Later that evening, after Sam had rung, Loveday had a shower and curled up on the sofa in her pyjamas and thick towelling robe, sipping a steaming mug of hot chocolate as she stared into the last glowing embers of the fire. She had come to a decision. She would make a few more enquiries of her own into Silas's death. But she had no intention of letting Laura know that.

15

The Crime Wall in the CID suite was filling up. Sam was perched on DC Malcolm Carter's desk as he and the rest of the murder team studied it. The picture of the tree in Bolger's Wood, and the grim sight of Silas Venning dangling on a rope from one of its branches, dominated the collection of photographs. There was another shot of those crudely carved initials, I and T, separated by a heart.

Sam's gaze travelled over the wall to the picture of Exeter Prison, and a separate image of the young Brian Penrose, which the man's parents had given Sam and Will. His eyes lingered on the image. He looked like a very ordinary young man, hardly the monster that Sam had built up in his mind, but he had to have a connection to all this. Sam just hadn't yet figured out what it was.

Also on the wall was a photograph of

Venning Marine, plus a couple of shots printed from the Internet of the murder victim, his widow Laura, and the couple's friend, Dr Meredith Deering. A photograph of the necklace Laura Venning had accused Loveday of stealing had also been pinned up.

DC Amanda Fox has been sent to obtain a photo of Liam Barnes and Danny Santos, and the pictures were now positioned by the side of the Venning Marine image.

Sam got up and stood by the wall. 'OK, let's concentrate, everyone. What are we seeing here?' He pointed to Danny Santos. 'We know he had a dust-up with Venning at his office in the boatyard, allegedly because he believed Silas Venning was responsible for having his friend, Brian Penrose, attacked in prison.' He glanced around the room. 'We only have this second-hand, of course.'

He turned to Amanda. 'You weren't able to track Santos down yesterday?'

She screwed up her face. 'Not exactly, sir, but I do know where he's been living. His mother took a lot of persuading, but when I eventually managed to convince her that he could help in our current investigation, she told me about this place out on Bodmin Moor. Apparently he's been hiding out there. She knew where it was because she'd taken food and a change of clothes to him.'

Amanda sighed. 'Following her directions, I found the place. It was a crumbling old stone hovel, but the doors and windows were intact, and the roof was there. Can't imagine it would be very comfortable, though.'

'D'you think he's still living there?' Sam's voice had an edge to it.

Amanda nodded. 'There were definite signs of habitation. I could see clothes strewn about the floor and the remains of takeaways.'

Sam's attention was still fixed on her. 'I did go back a couple of times, but . . . ' She shrugged, glancing to Santos' picture on the Crime Wall. 'Do you want me to go back there today, sir?'

'We'll both go,' Sam said.

Amanda nodded, keeping her expression noncommittal. She was hardly about to advertise the fact that the prospect of a couple of hours in the company of DI Sam Kitto wasn't at all displeasing to her.

Sam turned to Will. 'What about Liam Barnes? Anything interesting there?'

Will looked down, flicking through the pages of his notebook. 'Nothing much, boss. Before joining Venning Marine, he was a junior partner in Gill and Townsley in Plymouth.' He looked up. 'They're a firm of accountants.'

'He never mentioned anything about being an accountant when we spoke to him,' Sam frowned. He was remembering how forthcoming the man had been about the financial state of the company. He'd been more than eager to tell them it was failing. 'Pay him another visit, Will.' He looked around the room. 'And take DC Carter with you.'

16

Sam wasn't aware of the sidelong glances he was getting from the young detective constable sitting next to him in the passenger seat. Amanda could just about understand why her boss wasn't keen on her driving his own car. The old silver Lexus was his pride and joy, and he was very precious about it. But this was a police pool car, and yet he had still insisted on driving.

She glanced out at the passing fields. The A30 wasn't too busy. The bulk of the early-morning congestion had passed. Most people had reached their places of work by now. The current traffic was the next stage: lorries delivering their wares to shops and businesses, company reps on their way to see clients.

Amanda tried to concentrate on their efforts to find Danny Santos. Maybe, after successfully avoiding her yesterday he thought he was safe. In that case, they might find him in the run-down hovel where he had been hiding out. On the other hand, yesterday's visit could have spooked him, and he could have gone to ground somewhere else. She hoped that wouldn't be the case. The big detective next to her would not be happy if Danny disappeared, and neither would she.

Sam had his eyes fixed on the road ahead as they approached Bodmin Moor, but his mind was somewhere else. Loveday was up to something. He'd sensed it in her voice when he'd phoned her late last evening, in the way she had steered the conversation away from work. He hadn't been a DI all these years without being able to read body language, and voices had their body language as well: Loveday's skilful avoidance of describing her day was telling him a lot. The trouble was, he just wasn't sure of the details.

She'd been all for confronting Laura Venning when the results of the finger-print testing on the necklace came in, despite him warning her off. He'd told her not to approach the woman, that it was his responsibility now. But this was Loveday, and she didn't take kindly to being told what to do.

As last night's telephone conversation played out in his mind, he realized that he had been the one to do all the talking. But then Loveday was good at listening: she was a journalist, after all, and drawing information out of people without them even being aware of it was her stock in trade. He went over their chat in his head and was sure he'd said nothing about the case. And the only thing he had learned from her was that she'd had lunch with Cassie. It all sounded so innocent — too innocent.

He let his thoughts roam to earlier in the evening when he had called Jack and Maddie, before they went to bed. Their excitement at hearing from him had delighted him as it always did, but it also filled him with guilt. He didn't see his children nearly often enough. Plymouth wasn't that far away. He just needed to make more of an effort. When he'd confided his feelings to Loveday, she'd told him not to beat himself up about it, but she agreed that everyone would be happier if Sam saw more of his kids. The school holidays weren't far away. When they'd wound up this Venning case, perhaps he could take them away for a few days?

'We turn off just up here on the right, sir. There's a kind of underpass.' Amanda's voice brought him back to the moment. He forced thoughts of Loveday aside. He had to concentrate on the job in hand now.

They took the winding road through Bodmin Moor, passing isolated farms and hamlets. Sam followed Amanda's directions off the road and onto a bumpy track that wound its precarious way uphill.

'How the hell did you manage to find this place?' he asked, grimacing as the pool car bounced them unceremoniously over the rough terrain.

'Perseverance, sir.' Amanda grinned, pleased at the backhanded compliment. She pointed ahead. 'We can pull in just over there. Do you see? There's a clear patch past that gate.'

Sam followed her suggestion and

brought the car to a halt by the wooden bar gate, but still saw no signs of Danny Santos' rundown bolthole. They both got out, stretching and rubbing their backs. The wind whispered all around them, bending the rough grass. Sam tugged his collar up against the cold, breathing in the peaty smell of the moor.

'Bracing, isn't it?' Amanda said.

Sam's eyes scanned the horizon. His young DC was enjoying this. In the far distance he could see the remains of an old engine house. 'Please don't tell me that's it,' he said.

'No, sir.' Amanda laughed. 'It's just along here, in the dip on the other side of that slope. But it's only a footpath, so we have to walk.'

Sam glanced around the bleak landscape. He hoped Santos wouldn't try to make a break for it when they eventually did find him. His legs weren't up to chasing fit young men all over the Cornish countryside.

He could feel the damp begin to seep into his shoes as they reached the top of the ridge and looked down on the near-derelict stone building below. He'd been expecting an old cottage, but this looked more like an animal shelter. The walls appeared to be intact, but the rusty tin roof had seen better days. A sheet of old corrugated material had also been wedged across the open door space.

Sam looked back at Amanda. 'Santos has been living here?'

She nodded, out of breath from trying to keep up with Sam's long strides. 'That's what his mum says. And there was definitely someone dossing down there when I was here yesterday.' She pointed. 'For a start, that corrugated thing was propped up next to the doorway, not in front of it, and when I peeked through I could see a silver flask and the remains of takeaways.' She paused to catch her breath. 'Pizza boxes, Chinese food cartons, that kind of stuff.'

Sam stopped and looked around him. 'Well, I don't see any pizza boxes, or any sign of a car. So we can presume someone has been looking after him.'

'His mother, probably,' Amanda said. They closed the remaining distance between themselves and the shabby building in silence.

Sam put a finger to his lips, telling his DC to be as quiet as possible, and indicated that she should go round the back in case there was an unexpected escape route round there. As she crept away, Sam stood by the makeshift door.

'It's the police, Danny. We want to talk to you. Can you let me in?'

There was a panicked scrambling noise from within, and then scuffling, and loud voices. Sam raced round to the back of the building. Santos was spluttering and squirming face-down on the damp turf, and Amanda was on top of him, her knee firmly wedged in his back. Sam grinned down at the protesting man. 'Hello Danny. Going somewhere, were you?'

Danny squinted up at him. 'How do I know you're coppers?'

Sam pulled out his ID card and held it down to the man's face. 'Is that good enough for you? Now, DC Fox here will let you go if you promise to play nicely.'

'OK . . . OK,' Danny spluttered. 'Just tell her to get off me.'

213

Sam nodded to Amanda and she got up, brushing down her navy waterproof coat.

'Come back to the car with us, and then you can tell us what you're doing, hiding yourself away out here.'

They moved off single-file up the track, keeping Danny in the middle. Sam was glad to note the old pool car still retained some of its heat. Amanda bundled Danny into the back and climbed in after him. Sam sat in the driving seat, swivelling round so he could see them both.

'So,' he started. 'Why all the cloak-and-dagger stuff?'

'Because they want to kill me, of course.'

'Who does?'

'Venning's people.' Danny let out an exasperated sigh, as though he was dealing with idiots.

'Why do you think they want to kill you?'

'To shut me up.' He paused and took an uneasy glance around the car, as though he expected to see his persecutors emerge from behind the large rocks on the boulder-strewn moor.

'OK, let's start from the beginning, Danny. What is it that you know?' Sam's mind was scrolling back over what Loveday and Cassie had told him. Danny Santos had claimed to them that Silas Venning had been involved in some kind of drugs scam. But, more importantly, he'd insisted that Silas had ordered Brian Penrose's killing.

Danny was staring out over the moor. 'They'll kill me if I tell you.'

'If you were so frightened, then why did you talk to those two ladies down at Falmouth Marina?'

Danny looked up quickly, his tongue flicking out, wetting his lips. 'They told you, did they?'

'Well, of course they did. Isn't that why you confided in them? You wanted them to tell us.' Sam gave him a hard stare. 'So stop wasting our time, Danny. If what you know in any way involves Silas Venning's murder, then you need to tell us.' He waited, his gaze never leaving Santos' face.

The man frowned. 'I don't know about

215

that. But it was definitely Venning that had Brian attacked inside.' He sniffed and wiped his nose on the sleeve of his jacket. 'It was a warning; Brian had threatened to let the cat out of the bag. He was going to tell you lot what he knew about Venning Marine. They were seriously into drugs, and Brian knew all about it.'

He looked up at Sam. 'Look, OK, Brian and I were no angels, but we didn't do drugs. I didn't know anything about this business until after they had a go at Brian. They thought that beating him stupid would shut him up, but it did the opposite. It made him good and mad.'

Danny's head was full of images now, of Brian's bruised and bleeding face that day he'd been to visit him in Exeter Jail. He was remembering how the knuckles on his friend's fists had bulged white as he tried to control his anger. That was when he'd told him about the drugs business.

'How did Penrose know about the drugs?' Sam's voice was grim. Penrose was still the man who had driven a car while drunk, the man who had killed his lovely Tessa. He might not have wanted him dead, but he was far from having much sympathy for him.

'Brian worked for Venning Marine. He'd been doing some last-minute finishing work on one of the yachts that had just had its sea trials. Two men turned up, supposedly interested in buying it.' He paused. 'According to Brian, they looked too rough to be toffs, and there was no way they were there to buy an expensive yacht, so he watched them. He saw Liam Barnes handing over a package. He wasn't sure at first what it was, but they knew he'd seen it. He was taken into Silas Venning's office and questioned.'

Sam interrupted. 'Just a minute. Are you saying Barnes and Venning were both there?'

Danny shook his head. 'Only Barnes and the two men. They offered him money to keep his mouth shut. Brian was frightened, so he agreed, but he felt bad about it.

'A few weeks later, they told him they needed his help. They wanted him on board when one of the yachts did its trials. He didn't know at the time that it was part of Barnes's underhand dealings.' He paused for breath. 'During the trials, the yacht would rendezvous with another boat, and certain packages would be transferred. Brian didn't think they needed his help, he said it was all part of a deliberate plan to involve him. If he was part of the operation, he could hardly shop them, could he?'

Amanda had been listening silently to Santos' story, but now she spoke. 'When exactly did all this happen?'

Danny Santos sighed. 'A couple of months before he was jailed. You might say it was the reason he was jailed.'

Sam's head snapped up, but it was Amanda who asked what he meant.

'Brian got himself good and drunk this night. I was with him. I knew something was wrong, but he wouldn't say anything.' Danny heaved another sigh. 'I told him not to drive, but . . . '

'And he killed an innocent pedestrian,' Sam said.

Amanda shot him a look. Of course . . .

the DI's wife! She hadn't realized Brian Penrose was *that* drunk driver. She saw the muscles tighten in Sam's jaw and wanted to put her arms around him . . . to tell him everything was OK. But she knew she couldn't do that. She bent her head and said nothing.

17

Loveday spent most of the drive into Truro that morning working out how best to approach Meredith Deering. Sam had said nothing about suspecting her of killing Silas, and yet Laura had mentioned it. Was it just more game-playing on the woman's part? She wouldn't be surprised.

She quickly discarded any idea of appearing to meet Meredith by chance. That would look far too contrived. The last thing she wanted was to give the woman grounds for being suspicious about her. No, she would have to be much more inventive. She thought about simply calling her and asking for a meeting, but what justification would she have? In the end, fate took the whole thing out of her hands.

The Chiverton roundabout was even busier than usual that morning. The black Astra ahead had begun to move onto the roundabout when the driver suddenly slammed on his brakes. Loveday hit her own brakes, and the car screeched to a halt as the vehicle behind rammed into her Clio with a shuddering force. Her seatbelt saved her from slamming into the steering wheel, but the impact had inflated the car's safety bag, trapping Loveday in her seat. She felt sick. There was a dull pain in her back.

Within seconds, faces were appearing all around her as drivers left their vehicles and hurried to see what help they could offer. Someone was punching 999 into his mobile phone. The morning rush on the A30 had come to a complete standstill. Loveday felt a wave of nausea sweep over her. She forced herself to concentrate on breathing. Passing out now would not be a good thing. People were milling round her car now, and she was aware of the passenger door being opened.

'I'm a nurse,' a gentle female voice said as its owner climbed in beside her. 'Now, try not to move. Are you in much pain?'

Loveday winced. 'My hand hurts, it's . . . '

221

'It's all right. You've just got a little burn from the force of the safety bag inflating.'

The pain in her back was throbbing now. Loveday longed to stretch and just get out of the claustrophobic space, but her legs were so shaky that she knew she couldn't stand. She must have shifted, for the woman touched her arm and repeated her warning not to move.

'You could have a back injury,' she said gently. 'Best to keep as still as you can until the paramedics check you out.'

Loveday's body was beginning to ache quite painfully now, and the nausea was coming in waves. She closed her eyes. *Don't throw up*, she told herself. *Don't pass out*. She focused on breathing. The nurse's words were meant to be comforting, but they had the opposite effect. She tried not to think about the consequences of a back injury. From somewhere in the distance came the sound of an ambulance siren. In the driving mirror, she could see a buzz of activity around the mink-coloured Jaguar that had slammed into her. Her eyes narrowed as she tried to think if she had noticed it before the accident.

She hadn't, and the sleek, expensive Jag was not a vehicle easily overlooked. As far as Loveday could see, there was only one person in the car, and he was now slumped over the wheel, his body almost totally obscured by the inflated safety bag. He wasn't moving. Loveday bit her lip. 'The other driver . . . ' Her voice came out in a shaky whisper. 'Is he badly hurt?'

The young woman's glance lifted to the back window of Loveday's car, and she saw the concern in her grey eyes. 'He's being looked after,' she said quietly.

The sirens were louder now and Loveday could see the blinking blue lights of the ambulance.

'The paramedics are here,' the young woman said, giving Loveday a reassuring smile and a pat on her arm. 'You'll be fine now.'

'I don't know your name,' Loveday called out as the young woman turned to scramble out and make way for the paramedic.

She glanced back briefly. 'It's Beth,' she said.

Loveday tried a shaky smile. 'Thank you, Beth.'

Ten minutes later, Loveday was strapped onto a stretcher, a neck brace in place, and was being lifted into an ambulance. She closed her eyes as they raced through the busy city streets, sirens sounding. She could imagine the vehicles outside pulling over, making way for them. She had never been in the middle of such a situation before, and it was running through her mind that she needed to write about it — perhaps an article about the efficiency of the emergency services, and the Good Samaritan nurse who had sat with her and held her hand.

The back pain was easing off now, and the feelings of nausea were receding. Visions of the driver in the car that had crashed into her kept flashing through her mind. From the brief glimpse she'd got of him in her mirror after the accident, he had appeared to be unconscious. And the paramedics were still working on him back at the scene. *Please God, don't let him be dead*, she prayed silently as they wheeled her into the Truro hospital.

They were taking her for a scan when she heard her mobile phone ring. She began to look around for her bag when a firm hand was placed on her arm.

'Leave it,' said the nurse walking beside the trolley as it rumbled along the hospital corridor. 'You can ring whoever that is back when you've had your scan.'

Loveday took a deep breath and fixed her eyes on the row of lights moving past on the ceiling. The caller would be Keri. She'd be wondering where Loveday was. Or maybe it was Sam. She hated knowing how worried they would all be about her when they heard about this.

She glanced up at the nurse. 'Can someone find out how the other driver is?'

The nurse gave a brief smile. 'I'll ask. But for the moment, you just concentrate on yourself.'

'You will let me know, though?'

The nurse smiled again. 'Of course I will.'

Following the scan, Loveday had been put into a side ward while doctors examined her results.

'You've taken quite a knock, young lady,' said the tall, thin, grey-haired man in the blue-striped shirt and purple tie, as he strolled into the room clutching a tablet computer. He removed his spectacles. 'I'm Mr Giles, Orthopaedic Consultant.' He put one of the legs of his spectacles between his teeth. 'You have been lucky. Your back is not broken.' He looked down at her. 'In fact, you've escaped with only a few cuts and bruises.'

Loveday gulped. She had been trying to stay positive, but the fear of a back injury had terrified her. It was like this man had given her life back. She could feel tears of relief well up.

'No need for that, young lady,' the consultant said. 'You'll be fine now. We'll keep you here for a couple of hours, and if you feel well enough then you can go home.'

Loveday took another swallow. 'Thank you so much,' she said.

No one had yet come to tell her about the condition of the other driver, so she said, 'Do you know how the other person involved in my accident is?'

The consultant pursed his thin lips together. 'He's not as well as you. In fact, he will be spending a few weeks with us, but we're confident of a full recovery.'

'Really?' Loveday's face lit up.

The man nodded. 'Yes, really,' he said as he left the room.

Loveday's head sank back onto the bed. She'd been to hell and back today, and now she'd been told that everything was fine. The relief was overwhelming. Her eyes moved to the clock on the wall. It was almost noon — and none of the people she cared about even knew she was here. She had to ring Sam. She had to ring Keri and Merrick.

The nurse had put her bag into her bedside cabinet and she reached down to retrieve it, rummaging inside for her mobile phone. She found it and quickly scrolled down the list of missed calls. They were all there. Even Cassie had been trying to contact her. Her finger hovered over Sam's number.

18

Loveday had learned the name of her fellow accident victim from one of the nurses, and when she'd been told which ward he was in, she went in search of him. The first person she saw coming out of the ward was Meredith Deering. She wasn't sure which of them was the more surprised.

'Loveday! What are you doing here?'

Loveday glanced over her shoulder, checking out the rows of beds. 'I've come to enquire after Michael Clayton,' she said.

Meredith slipped her hands into the pockets of her white coat. 'You know Mr Clayton?'

'Not exactly,' Loveday said. 'We were involved in an accident this morning, and I just wondered how he was doing. Mr Giles, the consultant, gave me the impression that he had some serious injuries.'

'Mr Clayton's my patient, as it happens, but I'm afraid you won't be able to see him. We are only admitting close family.'

Loveday's face fell. 'Does that mean he really is serious?'

'I'm not at liberty to discuss my patients . . . sorry.' She paused for a moment, studying Loveday's face. 'I tell you what, I'm due a break about now. Do you fancy a coffee? The hospital canteen isn't great, but they do a fairly acceptable cappuccino.'

'I'd like that.' Loveday smiled.

The canteen was quiet when they arrived there, the lunchtime rush over. Meredith indicated a table and told Loveday to sit down while she fetched the coffees.

'Now, tell me about this accident,' she said when she got back with their drinks on a tray. Her green eyes were examining Loveday's bruised face.

Loveday described the shunting incident, mentioning the nurse who had held her hand until the ambulance arrived.

'Well, I'm glad you're not badly hurt.' Meredith took a sip of coffee and glanced

229

around. Loveday wondered if she was checking that no one was in earshot.

Meredith slipped off her stethoscope and coiled it into one of the large pockets in her white coat. 'How's the investigation into Silas's death going?' Her tone was conversational, but Loveday hadn't missed the woman's uneasy glance away.

'I've no idea. I'm not privy to that kind of police information. I'm not that kind of journalist.'

Meredith looked embarrassed. 'Sorry. I just wondered, with you being friendly with Inspector Kitto . . . '

'We are friends,' Loveday said. 'But he doesn't discuss his cases with me. I would imagine Laura might know more about that.'

Meredith cleared her throat. 'Laura and I don't see so much of each other any more. I think you can guess why.'

'You mean Silas? I'm sorry, Meredith, but I don't think you can really blame her. Her husband has just been murdered, and now she discovers that her best friend had been having an affair with him behind her back.'

Meredith frowned. 'Actually, I've been thinking about that, and I don't believe Silas and I were exactly a surprise to Laura.'

Loveday stared at her. 'Are you saying Laura knew about your affair?'

Meredith nodded. 'She knew what Silas was like. It wouldn't be difficult to put two and two together. She also knew that if it hadn't been me, it would have been some other woman. It was no secret that Silas liked to have his little flings.'

Loveday shook her head. 'I don't understand. If you knew what Silas was like, why did you . . . ?'

'I know.' Meredith threw her hands up in a helpless gesture. 'I should have had nothing to do with him, but Silas Venning was a very difficult man to refuse.' She gave a wistful smile. 'He was also quite endearing when he set his mind to it. Anyway, he wasn't the only one cheating on his marriage. Laura isn't exactly an angel either.'

Loveday blinked. 'What do you mean?' There seemed to be so many lies and tall stories being spun around this case that she didn't know who to believe.

'I'm talking about her and Liam Barnes,' Meredith said.

'Silas's right-hand man?' Loveday had suspected something might have been going on between the two of them. Laura had been too quick with her sharp criticism of him. She leaned forward, making sure no one else was in earshot. 'You think they were having an affair?'

'Why not? Now that Silas is out of the way, she can do what she likes.'

The spiteful tone in Meredith's voice made Loveday sit up again. Was she jealous of Laura and Liam? Did she fancy the man herself? And then she had another thought. 'Did Silas confide in you?'

'What do you mean?'

'Well . . . ' Loveday shifted in her chair. 'Did he tell you, for instance, that Venning Marine was in financial trouble?'

Meredith's brow wrinkled. 'Was it? I did wonder. Silas had been moody lately, but then he could be like that sometimes. Now that you mention it, though, it could have been something else. I know that recently Laura was meddling in the business a lot more than she usually did. Silas didn't like that.'

'Hang on,' Loveday said. 'I was under the impression that Laura took no interest in the business — at least, that's what she told me.'

Meredith gave a little laugh. 'She liked to keep under the radar, but the boatyard is Laura's business. It's her money that's behind it.'

Loveday needed to think. Had she been basing her assessments on completely wrong information? Had Laura deliberately misled her? But why? What did she have to gain? It could simply be that she didn't want to reveal too much to a journalist. She pursed her lips, giving this thought more consideration. Yes, that must be it. The interview for *Cornish Folk* was about Laura Anstey, the artist; not Laura Venning, wife of a business mogul. Perhaps she thought the Venning name would affect her artistic persona? One thing was certain, though. Laura Venning was a very manipulative woman.

She glanced across at Meredith. 'You said she was meddling in the business?

233

What kind of meddling?'

Meredith's pager went off and she fished it out of her pocket. 'I have to go, sorry.' She got up and flashed Loveday an apologetic smile.

'What about Mr Clayton?' she called out after her. 'I only want to see for myself that he's all right.'

Meredith spun round on her three-inch high heels. 'Two minutes. No longer.'

'Thanks, Doctor,' Loveday called after her as Meredith's heels clicked briskly out of the canteen and into the corridor.

Loveday retraced her steps back to Michael Clayton's ward. She found his room and glanced through the glass panel in the door. A nurse was checking the pulse of the grey-haired man who was sitting up in bed. Even in the basic hospital garment, the man looked distinguished. His expensively-cut silvery hair had been smartened into shape, and although his skin had a worrying grey pallor, he was smiling.

They both looked up as Loveday made her hesitant entrance. She flashed a reassuring smile. 'Dr Deering said I could have a minute with Mr Clayton.' The nurse glanced at her patient, who raised a questioning eyebrow at the newcomer.

Loveday thought about offering her hand, and then decided against it. 'You don't know me, Mr Clayton. My name is Loveday Ross . . . ' She hesitated. ' . . . from the accident?' Her voice went up an octave.

The man's quizzical frown disappeared as the realization dawned. 'You were the other driver?'

Loveday nodded.

'I'm so sorry,' he said. 'I have no excuses. I just don't know what happened.'

The nurse gave Loveday a warning look. 'Mr Clayton mustn't be upset.'

'This young woman is not upsetting me, nurse. I want to talk to her.'

The nurse pressed her lips together in disapproval, but relented. 'A few minutes only, then.'

Loveday waited until she had left the room before turning to Clayton. 'I just wanted to make sure you were OK. I'm not staying.'

'Please sit down, Miss Ross, and tell me

about the accident. The last I remember was being on the A30. I know I was coming to Truro, but the rest is a blank.'

'Please don't worry. It was only a shunting accident,' Loveday said, and then paused, not sure how much to tell him. She didn't want to be responsible for the man having another seizure. 'What have the doctors said?'

'I've been told I had a heart attack at the wheel.'

'You passed out.' She briefly described the incident, playing down the drama of the event. 'The important thing is that no one was seriously hurt.' She gave him a shy smile. 'Including yourself.'

Michael Clayton's head sank back onto the propped-up pillows. 'I can't even remember why I was coming into Truro.'

Loveday leaned over and covered his hand with hers. 'I shouldn't worry about it. I'm sure you will be feeling much better after a good rest.' She started to get up. 'Can I do anything for you? Contact anyone?'

The elderly man gave her a wistful smile. 'That's kind of you, my dear, but there's no one to tell. I lost my lovely wife, Evelyn, three years ago. The only other person who needs to know I am here is my business partner, and he has been informed.'

'What kind of business are you in?' Loveday asked before she could stop herself. She wasn't here to get the man's history. It was that journalist's curiosity working again.

'We run a boatyard in Penzance.' He smiled. 'We build luxury yachts.'

The pieces of the jigsaw were beginning to slot into place. Could this man's company be the same one that was giving Venning Marine such a bad timely lately? But she discarded the theory as soon as she'd thought of it. It would be too much of a coincidence. She glanced away. There were things she wanted to ask, but she didn't want to upset the old man.

'There is one thing you could do for me,' Michael Clayton's voice cut into her thoughts. 'Do you think you might come to visit me again? I'd like that.'

Loveday smiled. 'I'd love to, but I'm not sure what your doctor will think of that. It took all my powers of persuasion to get in to see you now.'

Michael waved away her comment with a feeble hand. 'Don't worry about Meredith. She always did fuss too much. I'm hardly likely to fade away because a charming lady pays me a visit.'

Loveday's eyebrow arched. 'You know Meredith? I mean, Dr Deering.'

Michael nodded. 'Since she was a baby. Meredith is my sister Victoria's child.' He sighed. 'My late sister.'

'So you're Meredith's uncle?' Loveday couldn't hide her astonishment. Michael Clayton gave her the kind of smile that showed what a handsome man he must have been in his youth.

She knew from Laura that the women had been childhood friends, so did this mean that Michael knew Laura? She took a breath. Nothing ventured . . . 'Did you know Laura Venning back then too?' But she already knew that he did. He must have.

'Of course I knew Laura, but her name was still Anstey then. My wife, Evelyn and I, were friendly with the Ansteys. We were members of the same sailing club. Meredith and Laura were inseparable. I wasn't always sure it was a healthy situation.'

Loveday lifted an eyebrow, and the old man sighed. 'Laura could be very dominating, even then, but Meredith thought the world of her . . . she still does.'

Michael's voice was becoming noticeably weaker. No matter how much Loveday wanted to know more about this relationship, she wouldn't encourage the man to talk at the detriment of his health.

She stood. 'I think you should try to get some rest, Mr Clayton.'

Michael's head sank back into the pillow. 'You haven't said you'll come back again yet.'

'I'll make a pact with you.' She smiled down at him. 'If you concentrate on getting fit again, then yes, of course I'll come back. And in the meantime, I'll ask one of the nurses to bring you one of my cards. It has my mobile number, so you can always reach me.'

He stretched out, offering his hand. 'I'd call that a deal.'

Loveday's head was buzzing as she headed back to her own little ward. The likeable, well-mannered man she'd just met didn't fit the image that had been in her head. From what she thought she knew about Clayton-Barratt, she had been picturing a slick, wheeler-dealer character, a man with plenty of front but no breeding, a man who had no scruples about destroying a competitor's business. The man who had just shaken her hand and asked her to visit him in his hospital bed was no wheeler-dealer. He was the genuine article — a gentleman. She wondered again if this man was the Clayton of Clayton-Barratt Boat Builders. She was confused. She needed time to get her thoughts in order.

Loveday was sure she had just been told something important; she just had to work out what it was, and how it fitted into the pattern of things. If Michael Clayton had been so friendly with Laura and her parents, then why was he trying to destroy Laura's yacht-building company? If that was even true. She was confused and her head was hurting. She concentrated on staying calm.

As she entered the ward, the nurse she recognized gave her a reproachful look. 'Where have you been? The consultant is on his way here to see you. He needs to give you one final check-over if you're to be discharged.'

Loveday had already made up her mind that she was going home. 'Sorry,' she said, in what she hoped was a suitably apologetic voice. 'I just needed to stretch my legs.'

The nurse gave her a look that said she didn't believe a word, but now wasn't the time to go into it.

The consultant arrived five minutes later and looked at Loveday over the top of his spectacles. He sighed. 'We should really keep you in overnight . . . '

Loveday's eyes flew open, but she didn't get the chance to cut in, telling him there was no need for an overnight stay.

Mr Giles raised a conciliatory hand. 'I was about to say that I knew you might raise a few objections to that.' He moved closer to Loveday, putting a stethoscope to her chest, examining her eyes, before straightening up again and turning to the nurse. 'Your patient can go home,' he said. He glanced back to Loveday with an unexpected smile. 'Just don't overdo things.'

Loveday assured him that she wouldn't, and with that the consultant was off, striding back out of the tiny room and marching along the corridor.

An hour later Loveday was sitting in the patients' waiting room, her eyes glued to the sliding doors for Sam's arrival. But it wasn't Sam who came to collect her. It was Cassie.

19

'Do you want to talk about it?' Cassie asked as they drove out of the hospital car park and headed for Marazion.

Loveday shrugged. 'Nothing much to say. It was a shunting accident. I was a bit shaken, but I'm fine now. My main concern is my car. Heaven knows how long it will be out of action.'

'Your car?' Cassie's voice rose incredulously. 'Your main concern is your car? You could have been killed!'

'Oh, Cassie, you do exaggerate. The poor man in the vehicle behind had a heart attack, and the accident was hardly his fault. He's the one we should be worried about.'

Cassie sighed. 'Have you any idea how anxious we've all been? You gave us quite a scare. Poor Sam still sounded as if he was in shock when he rang asking if I could pick you up. He hated being called away like that at the last minute.'

Loveday remembered how apologetic he'd been when he rang her mobile just as Cassie arrived. It was all she could do to convince him she didn't mind her friend giving her this lift. She was just relieved to be going back to the cottage.

'I wasn't sure what you had in,' Cassie went on, 'so I picked up a couple of steaks, some new potatoes and a bit of salad.'

Loveday's mouth fell open. 'You did that?'

Cassie kept her eyes on the road, but Loveday could see the corners of her mouth twitching in a smile.

She grinned at her. 'Cassie Trevillick . . . I swear you have wings and a halo tucked away somewhere in one of those big cupboards in your house.'

Cassie's face relaxed into an even broader smile. 'Just don't expect this treatment every night,' she said.

The clock on a church tower chimed four as they drove past a sign to Tregarth. It was the name of the village Sam had mentioned, the one where her Clio had been towed for repair. It suddenly struck

244

Loveday that the garage would still be open. If they stopped off there, at least she could get an idea of how long the repairs might take.

Loveday put on her most persuasive voice. 'Would you mind going back and stopping for a few minutes, Cassie, while I just check up on the car?'

'Sam told me to take you straight home.'

'Please, Cassie . . . '

Cassie sighed. 'OK, where is this place?'

It was another ten minutes before they pulled up outside Lime Tree Garage. Loveday winced as she climbed down from the Land Rover. She was still feeling stiff and sore. Merrick's advice to take time off was good, but she wouldn't be putting her feet up. She had already planned what work she could do from home.

A man in a dirt-smudged navy boiler-suit emerged onto the garage forecourt, wiping his hands on an oily rag. 'What can I do for you ladies?' he said, glancing at Cassie's gleaming vehicle.

Loveday introduced them both.

The man stuck out his hand and then

withdrew it quickly, remembering how greasy it was. 'Tim Gordon, sole proprietor of this great enterprise.' He took an exaggerated glance around the place, and then grinned at them.

'My car was in an accident this morning,' Loveday started to explain, and then spotted her Clio up on a ramp.

'Oh, it's yours, is it? Well, you were lucky.' The mechanic glanced back at her car. 'She's taken a bit of a knock, but it could have been a lot worse. You'll need new back and front bumpers, of course, but they shouldn't take too long to fit.'

'So I might be able to pick it up in the next day or two?' Loveday raised a hopeful eyebrow.

'You'll be lucky. I haven't sent off for the new parts yet.' He rolled his eyes to the garage's corrugated metal roof. 'Shouldn't take more than a day or two for them to come, though, and then depending what else I have on, another day or so to fit.'

He ignored Loveday's sigh. 'Think yourself lucky, love. The other car came off far worse.' He peered back into the dark interior of the garage, where Loveday could just make out the lines of a Jaguar.

She nodded towards it. 'Is that the other vehicle from the accident?'

The mechanic frowned. 'Yeah, it's in a right mess . . . no brake fluid, you see.'

Loveday was still staring at Michael Clayton's car. Even in this sad state, it had a look of a vehicle that was well looked-after. How could Michael, or whoever looked after his car, have failed to have the brake fluid checked?

'Isn't that a bit unusual?' she said.

Tim's oil-streaked face stretched into a grimace. 'For a motor like that one, it is. The lead was nicked, not enough for the brake fluid to drain away all at once, but enough for it to trickle out — which is what it did.'

He scratched his head. The other person who had called in earlier that afternoon enquiring after the Jag had made him think. If he didn't know better, he would have said someone had deliberately . . . But that was dangerous thinking. Still, maybe he should give the police a call, just to keep himself in the clear.

Loveday had been watching the man's face intently. He was thinking there was something suspicious about this too. She was sure of it.

'Could the car have been tampered with?' she asked.

Cassie threw her an appalled look. 'For heaven's sake, Loveday . . . '

'Well,' she persisted, holding the man's hesitant stare, 'could someone have interfered with the Jag?'

Tim Gordon's eyes were guarded. If there was something funny going on here, he didn't want to get involved in it. But he'd made up his mind. He wouldn't discuss his suspicions with these women. He would ring the coppers.

Loveday read the man's mind. He was suspicious all right. And so was she now!

A ripple of ice swept through her veins. The accident hadn't been caused by Michael Clayton having a heart attack. He had had a heart attack because someone had sabotaged his car. Someone had deliberately tried to kill Michael

248

Clayton. But why?

Cassie had been eyeing Loveday warily, and knew exactly what was now going through her mind. She put a hand on Loveday's arm, turning her back in the direction of the Range Rover.

'We'll keep in touch, Mr Gordon,' she called over her shoulder to the mechanic as they left.

'Did you hear what he said, Cassie?' Loveday asked, as soon as they had got back in the vehicle.

'Yes I did, and if there is any truth in it then it's for Sam to deal with.' She gave her friend a warning look as she started the engine and pulled out onto the road. 'And don't for a minute consider getting yourself involved here, Loveday. You have quite enough on your plate for the time being.'

20

Sam's eye strayed once again to the clock on the wall of the interview room. It was almost five. Cassie would have picked Loveday up from the hospital by now. It should have been him driving her home. It wasn't for the first time that he cursed the job, but there was no way he could have left, not after Jesse Vance had presented himself at the front desk demanding to see him. The last time they'd had him in one of the station's interview rooms, he'd refused to talk; and since they had no good reason to detain him, he'd been allowed to leave.

The man had obviously had a change of heart since, and had turned up at the front counter offering to make a statement. The subsequent interview proved surprisingly informative, so much so that the man had stopped it mid-stream and demanded to see a solicitor.

Hannah Galt, the duty solicitor, had

arrived with an air of harassment, looking nothing like anyone's idea of a solicitor. Small, rosy-cheeked, and with thick, wiry auburn hair that was pulled back from her face and secured at the nape of her neck with a clip, she looked up at Sam with keen blue eyes before thrusting out a hand. 'Hannah Galt,' she informed him. 'I believe you have a client for me, Inspector.'

Sam and Will had waited impatiently while Jesse and Hannah Galt talked for more than an hour in private.

'This is ridiculous,' Sam muttered, and was about to call the solicitor out and demand to know how much longer they would be when the door of the room they were occupying opened. He gave the young lawyer his no-nonsense look and said, 'I take it was can now interview your client, Ms Galt?'

She nodded as the great bulk of Jesse Vance appeared behind her. Sam led the way back to the interview room, beckoning for everyone to follow.

The metal frames of the chairs scraped on the stone floor as they took their seats, and Will set up the tape recorder again.

Solicitor and client waited for Sam to speak, but he said nothing, taking his time studying Vance's increasingly agitated expression.

Helen Galt fidgeted and looked at her watch. 'Can we get on with this, Inspector?'

Sam leaned forward, locking eyes with Vance. 'Tell us about your job with Venning Marine, Jesse . . . your *real* job I mean.'

Vance shot a nervous glance to his solicitor, and she nodded.

'I collected the drugs.' His beefy shoulders lifted in a shrug. 'It was good money, and it wasn't as if I was selling the stuff.'

Sam and Will exchanged grim glances. 'Go on,' Sam said.

For the next hour, the two officers tried to disguise their shock as Jesse Vance described Venning Marine's two-year involvement with a gang of Colombian drug runners, smuggling packages of cocaine into Cornwall.

They listened as he described how he sailed on new yachts — sometimes with

Liam Barnes at the helm, sometimes Venning himself — to pick up plastic-encased packages of drugs that had been dropped in the Channel at marked locations. The yachts were supposedly on sea trials, and no one ever questioned the trips.

Occasionally the routine changed, Vance said; they would rendezvous with another boat, and the drugs would be handed over that way.

Sam cleared his throat. 'What happened to the drugs?'

'They were brought back to the boatyard . . . stayed on board until they were collected.'

'Who collected them?' Will cut in.

'No idea. It wasn't part of my job to know that, and I didn't want to. I was just to keep an eye on the goods until they were picked up.' He put up a hand. 'And don't ask me where they went after that. Use your imagination. It's a big country . . . ' He reached for the bottle of water Sam had brought with him and placed on the table. 'Anyway, it was all threatening to fall apart when Penrose started shouting his mouth off.'

'Is that why Silas had him killed?' Sam asked.

Vance took a noisy gulp of water and wiped the back of his fleshy hand across his mouth. 'Don't know who ordered Penrose to be taken out. Might have been Venning. They were hardly going to tell me, now, were they?'

'Who did the killing?'

Vance raised his huge shoulders. 'Some local junkie. How do I know?' He took another noisy slug of the water. 'But Danny Santos was next in line. Penrose told him about the drugs, so he had to be silenced.' He looked up and gave Sam a chilling grin. 'Except Venning was the one who got himself silenced.'

Sam leaned forward, forcing Vance to meet his glare. 'Was that you, Jesse? Was it you who killed Silas?' Sam didn't really think the big man had been involved in Venning's murder, but he might know who was.

Vance scowled at him, his eyes bulging with rage. '*I* didn't bloody kill him,' he yelled back. 'Speak to Barnes about that.'

It was enough to have the man arrested. If Jesse Vance was telling the truth — and Sam was sure that he was — then the super-smooth Liam Barnes had a lot of explaining to do.

Jesse Vance was in a police cell, having been charged with a series of drug-related offences, as Will and Sam drove to the address in Restronguet that Liam Barnes had given in his written statement.

It was a pretty cottage down by the water, with a dinghy tied up at a mooring. There was no sign of a car, and no answer when they knocked. But they would return, and keep on returning until they found the man.

As they drove back to the station, the events of the past days raced through Sam's mind. They might be on the brink of shutting down a major drug-smuggling operation in Cornwall, as well as solving the murders of Silas Venning and Brian Penrose, but he had the uneasy feeling that not everyone in the force would be entirely happy about it.

How could cocaine have been smuggled in and out of Cornwall for two years without them knowing a thing about it? Questions would be asked, fingers pointed, blame laid. Sam needed to make sure that it wasn't laid at the door of his team. Officers from the Border Force Agency would be all over this now, but if they had been on the ball they would have already known about this. They would have been watching this gang. So why weren't they?

* * *

Loveday had been listening for Sam's car. At the familiar sound of its engine purring up the drive, she was out of her chair and rushing to throw open the door. Sam's broad smile as he sprang out of the Lexus and covered the space between them in three strides, sweeping her into his arms, made Loveday's heart pound.

'I'm so sorry I couldn't pick you up from the hospital. I . . . '

Loveday put a finger to his lips. 'You don't have to apologize, Sam. I understand. Anyway, Cassie brought me back.'

He lifted her chin, examining the bruise on her head. 'That looks painful.

Are you sure you were fit enough to come home?'

'Fit enough to cook us some supper.' She grinned up at him, standing on tiptoe to look over Sam's shoulder to the cooker. 'Cassie laid on some food for us. How does steak, chips and salad sound?'

'Heaven,' Sam said. 'It sounds like heaven.'

Loveday laughed. 'Would that make me an angel if I cooked it?'

He shook his head. 'I'll be the angel doing the cooking tonight. You go and sit by the fire.' He gave her the kind of grin that melted her heart, adding, 'And that's an order.'

Loveday had no quarrel with that. She went back to her armchair, stretching luxuriously as Sam got busy in the kitchen. She heard the clink of glasses, and he appeared seconds later with two large goblets of the red wine he had brought with him.

He handed one to her and put the other to his nose with an air of knowledgeable satisfaction. 'It's French,' he said. 'From the Rhône Valley.' He held up the glass, gazing into the deep ruby-red colour. 'A pleasing medium-bodied Crozes-Hermitage.'

'Did you just make that up?' She narrowed her eyes at him, but guessed he'd probably read it on the label. 'I didn't realize you were such a wine expert.' She accepted the proffered glass and took a sip of the delicious contents.

Sam gave a little bow. 'Does it meet with Madam's approval?'

'It's just perfect,' Loveday murmured, settling back contentedly into her chair. The cosiness of the fire, the effect of the wine, and the delicious aromas coming from the kitchen were putting Loveday in a wonderfully mellow frame of mind. She knew she had to mention her fears that Michael Clayton's Jag had been tampered with, but she had to choose her moment. She didn't want to risk Sam accusing her of interfering in his case again. Not tonight.

She waited until they had eaten their steak supper from trays in front of the fire, and made sure that Sam's glass was charged before relating her meeting with

Michael Clayton.

At the mention of the man's name, Sam's eyes narrowed. 'Not the boatyard Clayton . . . from Penzance?'

Loveday nodded. 'There's more.' She paused, looking across at him. 'He's Meredith Deering's uncle.' She watched his eyes work as he considered this. A coincidence? She knew Sam didn't like coincidences. Now that she had started she had to tell him the rest. She went on, 'Cassie and I called in at the garage on the way home. It will be a few days before I can have the Clio back. They have to send off for new bumpers.'

Sam gave a distracted nod. Loveday was trying to keep her tone conversational. Maybe the mechanic had already phoned Sam. She took a breath. 'Clayton's Jag was there, too. The thing is, Sam . . . ' She waited until she had his full attention. 'The mechanic I spoke to thinks it might have been tampered with.'

Sam's brow had creased into a deep frown.

She swallowed. 'Did he phone you?'

He was giving her a steely stare. 'No

. . . He didn't call me.'

Loveday sighed. 'He found a cut in the lead for the brake fluid thingy . . . and the brake fluid had been slowly draining away.' She met his eyes. 'He wasn't saying it was deliberate. It could have been an accident . . . ' Her voice trailed off.

'Why didn't you mention this earlier?' Sam put his glass on the table next to him and jumped up to find his phone. He was back in stern detective mode. Within minutes he had organized the seizure of Michael Clayton's Jaguar for further investigation, and mentally placed a visit to the Truro hospital on the following morning's itinerary.

21

It hadn't been a great weekend. Sam's mood had deteriorated after Loveday told him Michael Clayton's car could have been tampered with. She'd had the distinct impression that he wanted to leave there and then, and had only stayed the night to reassure her after the accident.

She could tell there had been some kind of big breakthrough in the case, but no matter how she tried to wheedle information out of him, Sam was keeping his mouth shut.

On Saturday morning he'd got up with the lark and gone off without any breakfast, leaving Loveday with a cup of coffee, a quick peck on the cheek, and a promise to keep in touch. Throughout the weekend there had been a succession of quick 'catch-up' phone calls, but Sam hadn't returned to Marazion.

The only plus point of the weekend was

the car Sam borrowed from a work colleague to keep her mobile while the Clio was being repaired. It was an old red Mini, and a bit of a boneshaker, but at least it was transport.

A black cloud hung over Loveday's mood as she returned to the office on Monday morning. Merrick had eyed her with doubt, asking if she was sure she was fit enough to come back to work. She insisted she was.

After checking her diary, arranging her day — and assuring the rest of her colleagues at the magazine that she really was back to full fitness after the accident — Loveday went off to her first appointment. It was an interview with a woman from Padstow who had launched a new app for Cornish walks. On the way back she had a text message from Michael Clayton, asking her to visit him in hospital as soon as she could.

Her first thought was that he'd had a relapse, but if that were the case then *he* would hardly be sending the text. Maybe he had some good news to share? But as soon as she walked into his room and saw his pale, drawn face, she knew that wasn't the case. Michael's skin was the colour of parchment, and Loveday was shocked by how fragile he looked.

Could Sam's questioning him about his car be responsible for his current condition? Was he fretting about the possibility that someone might have tried to kill him? But she quickly dismissed this. She knew Sam would have been gentle with his questions, so surely the old man hadn't been brooding about that.

'How are you, Michael?' she said quietly, taking the seat by his bed.

He reached out for her hand. 'It's Meredith. Something's happened, I know it has. She hasn't been to see me all weekend.'

Loveday frowned. She hadn't been expecting this.

'She was supposed to be on duty over the weekend, but she never turned up. The staff don't know where she is.' His grip on Loveday's hand tightened. 'I'm so worried about her.'

Loveday could feel an edge of disquiet flickering in her own stomach. She didn't like the sound of this. She had planned to seek Meredith out that morning to confront her about why she hadn't mentioned she was related to Michael Clayton. She'd had plenty of opportunity. Loveday's mind played over their conversation. There had been no hint that she was going away. Anyway, if she had been planning a trip she hardly needed to tell Loveday, but she would surely have told her uncle. She certainly wouldn't have upset him by just disappearing. Would she . . . ?

'Meredith could have been called away at the last minute . . . and then . . . well, she's probably just got detained somewhere,' Loveday said hesitantly. As possibilities went, this was as weak as they came — and Michael Clayton saw straight through it.

'I know you're trying to make me feel better, but even you can't believe that. Something's happened to Meredith. I know it.'

'When was the last time you saw her?' Loveday asked.

'Friday evening. She called in after her

264

shift had finished. She said she'd be back in the morning, but . . . '

Loveday gave his hand a pat. 'It's OK. Don't worry. We'll find her.'

'There *is* something you can do for me. Can you ask Laura if she knows anything? If Meredith is in trouble she might have confided in Laura. Will you go and see her, Loveday? Will you do this for me?'

Loveday forced a smile. The last thing she wanted to do right now was pay another visit to Laura Venning, but the word *disappeared* kept flashing through her mind all the way back to the office. Was that what had happened? Had Meredith disappeared? Would Laura really be able to shed any light on the mystery?

She rang Sam on his mobile. If Meredith had been reported missing, then he might have some news of her, but the thing went on to 'answer' and she didn't leave a message. Sam would probably just tick her off for meddling again.

* * *

265

Loveday took the winding, narrow road to Laura Venning's house at a slow pace that afternoon. She wasn't at all sure she was doing the right thing. What if Laura knew nothing of Meredith's whereabouts? The woman was so volatile that there was no telling how she might react to the news that her friend was missing.

She thought of making a U-turn in the borrowed Mini as soon as the road opened up closer to the big house. She'd promised to make enquiries on Michael's behalf, but she owed this woman no favours. She was still smarting with anger at how Laura had tried to set her up as a thief.

The explanation she'd offered, of only doing it to get Loveday on side to investigate Silas's death, was ludicrous. No sane person would . . . She stopped short. That was it. That was the thing that had been at the back of Loveday's mind all along. No sane person would behave like this. Perhaps Silas's death . . . his murder . . . had affected Laura more than she'd admitted. And then the man's affair with her best friend, Meredith. No matter what little dalliances Laura herself enjoyed, she must have felt so betrayed by both of them.

From the little Sam *had* mentioned about the latest developments in the case, and what Laura herself had revealed, Loveday knew that Venning Marine was in financial trouble, which would of course explain why they were involved in smuggling drugs.

She parked at the side of the big house and sat in the car, thinking. Her mind was ticking over all the things that had happened. First there was the discovery of Silas's body — initially thought to have been a suicide, but now definitely being treated as murder — and then the revelation that the two people closest to Laura had been cheating on her behind her back.

Next there was the hit-and-run outside Exeter Jail when Brian Penrose had been killed — right in front of Sam! She winced at the thought of how badly that must have affected him.

People were dying, and they were all connected to Laura's late husband — and

Venning Marine. She wondered what would distress Laura most. Would it be Silas's infidelity? But she must have been used to that, although perhaps not with her best friend. How would she react when she learned that the company had been involved in drug smuggling? She couldn't have been part of that, Loveday reasoned, because the woman had a fortune of her own. She was certainly obsessing about who could have murdered her husband. But why couldn't she leave that to the police? Why was she so insistent on involving her?

Loveday went over all the possibilities in her mind, but no matter which way she looked at it, things didn't make sense . . . unless — but no, that was a crazy idea. However, the more she thought about it, the more she convinced herself she could be right. Liam Barnes! Venning Marine's accountant. The man Laura had told her would be visiting the last time she'd been to Trevore. The man who was now running her husband's company. Did Laura suspect Liam Barnes of murdering her husband?

Another even more wild idea was beginning to take shape in her head. What if Barnes and Laura were lovers? What if she *knew* he had murdered Silas and was using her to set someone else up for the killing? Was the woman capable of such deviance?

There were no other vehicles parked in front of the big house as Loveday drove up and glanced around. Trevore was built to be a rich man's palace, the kind of place where people partied, where music and laughter drifted out onto the lawn. Today it looked desolate as she got out of the car and ran up the few steps to ring the bell.

She waited as the ringing echoed through the big white hall beyond . . . and then she heard the sound of footsteps. She'd been expecting to see the elderly maid as the door swung open, but it was Laura Venning herself who stood there.

Loveday almost didn't recognize the dishevelled creature standing in front of her. Laura was wearing a grubby, grey, paint-smeared cotton kaftan. Her hair, normally so sleek and silky, was a tousled mess, and there was a wildness in her glittering dark eyes.

She gave Loveday a bewildered frown. 'I didn't ask you to call,' she snapped. 'What do you want?'

It was the first time Loveday had seen the woman look flustered. It made her wonder what she had been doing before she rang the bell. But Laura recovered her composure so swiftly that Loveday thought she might have misjudged her first impression. The woman lifted her chin, and her face took on the haughty expression Loveday was more familiar with. 'I wasn't expecting you.'

'Can I come in, Laura?'

'Yes, of course. Come in.' She stepped back, allowing Loveday to enter. 'I'm in the drawing room. I think you know the way.'

Loveday did. She needed to make sure Meredith wasn't here, while at the same time not distressing the woman further. The two were close friends, after all, and if she didn't know where Meredith was, or even that she was missing, the news was undoubtedly going to upset her.

She glanced around, hoping to see the tell-tale signs that Laura had a visitor — and crossing her fingers that it wouldn't be Liam Barnes — but there were no signs that Laura had company. In fact, the room didn't look as though anyone had actually occupied it that day. No tea tray or coffee mug was in evidence, and there were no newspapers or magazines lying about . . . not even a glass of the vodka that Laura had seemed so fond of.

'I think you should sit down, Laura,' Loveday said gently.

The woman's eyebrow went up, no doubt surprised at being told what to do in her own home. But she sat anyway.

'Have the police been in touch with you?' It was a long shot, but someone at the hospital might have reported Meredith missing. Given the doctor's involvement in the Silas Venning case, Sam would have taken it seriously.

Laura leapt to her feet, her eyes glittering with anticipation. 'They've found something? Tell me! Have they arrested Silas's killer?'

'I'm sorry, Laura. I don't have any information about that. I . . . I just wondered if you've heard from Meredith?'

This wasn't coming out as she had planned. A look of irritation flickered in Laura's eyes.

'The police rang me earlier and asked the same thing.' She shrugged. 'I'm not privy to Meredith's private life . . . not any more. I don't even know who her friends are now.'

The woman sounded so sad that Loveday moved forward to touch her arm. Laura didn't seem to notice. 'There was a time when we told each other everything.' She shook her head. 'But not now. Meredith has her own life, and I'm no longer a part of it.'

Loveday watched Laura get up and go to pour herself a drink. She didn't offer Loveday one. It was as though she had forgotten she was there. 'You think you know someone . . . ' She was pouring a large measure of vodka into a tumbler. ' . . . and then they just turn their back on you.'

Loveday wasn't sure how to respond to

this, or even if she should. Laura had obviously been more deeply affected by her friend's betrayal with her husband than by any worries about her disappearance. The woman needed help, but Loveday wasn't sure she was the one to give it. It was professional help she needed.

'We were inseparable when we were children.' Laura turned back to face Loveday. 'Did you know that?' Loveday got the impression of a slight stumble as Laura paced back and forward to the large picture windows. Clearly this wasn't her first drink of the day after all.

'There was a treehouse at the bottom of the garden. It was our den.' Laura was speaking wistfully again; a sad smile curved her mouth. 'We played doctors and nurses. Meredith liked that. Even back then she wanted to be a doctor . . . to work in a hospital. We both did.'

Loveday thought it a strange choice of phrase. Surely most people would chose such a caring profession with the singular aim of helping people? Working in a hospital would be purely incidental.

'Meredith's uncle Michael made two little beds for her dolls. She fussed over them. They were her patients, you see.' She suddenly turned her attention on Loveday. 'Did you have dolls? I didn't. I had fishing rods. There was a stream at the end of the garden, where we caught . . . where I caught . . . '

She didn't finish the sentence. She lifted the glass and drained it, apparently unaware that her speech was becoming more and more slurred. 'She was too good to come fishing with me, but she ate the trout I caught. She'd do that all right. She helped build the campfire, but it was always me who had to cook the fish.' Her eyes were glazing over as she remembered. 'Some nightsh we were allowed to shleep in the tree house. We'd cuddle up to keep eassh other warm.' She wrapped her arms around herself.'

'Sounds like you two were very close.'

Laura gave a vigorous nod. 'Clossh . . . yessh, that's it. We were clossh.'

'And are you still close?' Loveday asked gently.

Laura was standing with her back to

274

her, looking out across the river. Her back went rigid. 'We could have been fine. It could have worked. It *would* have worked if Silas hadn't set his lecherous sights on her.'

The slur had gone. Loveday could see the woman's head slowly shake. 'He spoiled everything. Meredith and I were happy. Why couldn't he have left us alone? We weren't harming anybody.' She spun round, her eyes full of vengeful tears. 'We loved each other. We were going to be together forever, just Meredith and me — and then *he* had to spoil everything.'

22

Loveday stared at her. Laura and Meredith . . . a couple? Why had she not realized this? It answered so many questions. It explained why Laura appeared to have no real affection for her late husband, and no real grief at his death. An icy band of suspicion was beginning to weave its way through her insides.

Laura was watching her. Her mood had changed. She crossed the floor in unsteady strides, and thrust her angry face to within inches of Loveday's. Loveday tried to back away, but Laura grabbed her arm. 'You're very concerned about Meredith all of a sudden, aren't you, missy? Now, why would that be?' Her wild-eyed glare was only inches away.

Loveday shrunk back from the madness in Laura Venning's eyes. She swallowed, but her voice still came out in a croak. 'Is Meredith here?'

Laura's top lip curled in distaste as she

stepped back, glaring at Loveday. 'I get it now. You're after her too, aren't you? That's why you're here. You've got your eye on my Meredith.' She turned and began pacing the room. 'I should have known. It's so obvious now. You want Meredith for yourself.'

Loveday stared at her with wide-eyed shock. She shook her head. 'Of course I don't. I . . . ' She had started to tell her about Sam. Then decided that was none of this madwoman's business. 'I'll ask you again, Laura. Is Meredith here?'

'You want to see her? You want to see Meredith?' A cold smile slid across Laura Venning's face.

Loveday pushed past her and ran into the hall. She headed for the stairs with Laura in pursuit. 'Where is she, Laura?' she yelled over her shoulder.

She reached the studio, and burst in. The room was empty.

Wheeling round, she faced the other woman accusingly.

'I know that Meredith Deering is in this house.'

Laura's shoulder rose in a shrug. 'I

don't know what you're talking about.' She peered into Loveday's face. 'Are you feeling all right?'

Loveday was trying to control her shock and anger. 'Stop lying,' she shouted. 'Where is Meredith?'

Laura lifted her head and met Loveday's angry glare. In that split second, the woman's attitude changed. She narrowed her eyes. 'You're clever, Loveday Ross. I'll grant you that. What makes you think your little friend is here?'

'I know she is. And I know what you've done. Meredith didn't kill Silas, did she, Laura?' She took a step closer. Her insides were trembling. 'It was you all the time, wasn't it?'

Laura reached into the pocket of her paint-streaked kaftan — and produced a small handgun.

Loveday gasped. 'No, Laura! Put the gun down! You don't need that.'

She was trying to sound assertive, in control, but her voice was shaking.

'You made a big mistake coming here,' Laura said coldly, waving the gun in the direction of the big French windows.

278

'Now I have two of you to deal with.'

Loveday backed away.

'Open it,' Laura ordered. 'Open the window.'

Loveday fumbled with the handle, at last releasing the catch, and the doors swung open. A sharp breeze hit her face, and she realized there was a balcony outside — and a very long drop to a concrete path below. Frantically, she scanned the river, but she could see no boats. There was no one out there to help her.

Laura continued her menacing advance, flicking the gun in Loveday's face. A terrifying vision of her own body, broken and bleeding, sprawled on that path below, flashed through her mind. She shuddered.

Laura tut-tutted. 'Such a nuisance, you being so stupid. We were getting on so nicely, too.'

Loveday put up her hands. 'It's not too late to stop all this. Just tell me what you've done with Meredith.'

Laura had backed her out onto the balcony. Loveday's back was now pressing against the rail. She glanced down and saw the wooden doors of what looked like a boathouse flung open.

Laura's face was close. Loveday could feel the cold steel of the gun barrel next to her cheek.

'Put the gun away,' she pleaded. '*Please*, Laura.'

She heard the click of the gun's release mechanism, and shrank back. She was staring into the eyes of a madwoman!

With one quick flick of her wrist, Laura lashed the barrel of the pistol across Loveday's cheeks. There was a clatter as the gun flew out of Laura's hand, landing on the stone path below.

For a second Loveday saw stars, and felt herself slide down the railings. When she came to, her face was throbbing. She touched her cheek and her fingers came away covered in blood. She sat there for a few moments, trying to gather her thoughts. She didn't think she'd been shot, but she couldn't quite remember.

There was a loud grating noise on the stone path below, and Loveday twisted round to see what it was. She paused, her heart beating fast, and listened. There it was again — that noise. The realization of what it was came to her in a rush. It was the doors of the boathouse down below. Someone was closing them.

Loveday levered herself into a standing position and fished her mobile phone out of her pocket. She punched in Sam's number. It rang a couple of times and then went onto answerphone.

'I'm at Laura Venning's place, Sam,' she gasped into the phone. 'She has a gun. The woman's gone mad. Please hurry.'

Shakily, she moved towards the stairs, and slowly made her way down into the hall. She could see an open door in the furthest corner. She should wait for Sam to get here, but if she did it might be too late. Meredith could be dead right now for all she knew.

Heart pounding, she moved stealthily towards the door, and then stopped. She was gazing down a flight of stairs leading to a cellar. The Vennings must have had this cellar converted to a boathouse. It made sense, given this couple's involvement in all things yachty. Loveday could see a light at the bottom of the stone steps. Her knees trembled as she crept on.

Someone was down there: she could hear a scuffing noise as though something was being dragged across a stone floor. She swallowed back a wave of nausea. Was it Meredith? She was remembering how the gun had clattered on the path below the upstairs drawing room. With a feeling of dismay, she realized it had probably landed right beside the boat-house. Laura probably had it in her hand right now. Had she already used it on Meredith? Had Laura already killed her?

Loveday reached the bottom step, forcing herself to take deep, silent breaths. She moved as if in slow motion, cautiously craning her neck to peer round the corner to where she'd heard the sounds.

Only one of the double doors had been closed, and although the inside of the boathouse was gloomy, the scene was all too clear. She gasped. Laura was curled up on the stone floor, her hands and feet lashed with a thick rope. She was not moving. Meredith was standing over her, pushing her hands through her long, damp blonde hair. Her head jerked up in panic as she saw Loveday.

'Thank God you're safe, Meredith. You know she had a gun?' Loveday moved forward, put out a reassuring hand. 'Did she hurt you?

Meredith gave her a stunned stare.

The woman was certainly dishevelled, but Loveday couldn't see any bruises or blood. She glanced down to Laura. She was very still. Squatting down, Loveday checked her pulse. It was very faint. 'We need to get Laura to hospital.'

Meredith didn't move. She locked eyes with her.

'Now!' Loveday said sharply.

But Meredith remained motionless . . . staring.

Loveday decided she was in shock, and reached into her pocket for her phone to punch in the triple nine. She'd just hit the final digit on the keypad when Meredith let out a roar and lunged forward, knocking the phone from her hand and kicking it out of reach.

Loveday eyed her with disbelief. 'What are you doing? We need to get help.'

For a split second, Loveday thought the kidnapping ordeal had temporarily affected

Meredith's judgment. But this was more than that. She glanced back to Laura, and for the first time saw the dark wet patch of matted hair. Her eyes flew across the floor to her phone. Had she connected with 999? She didn't know. She could only hope that help was on the way.

'Meredith.' She spoke as loudly as she dared. 'You could have killed Laura. The longer she's tied up here on the floor, the worse it will be. You can't just come into someone's home and — '

'Shut up . . . shut up!' Meredith screamed. She reached into the pocket of her coat and produced a familiar-looking gun.

Loveday flinched; the feeling of *déjà vu* was sickeningly real. 'What are you doing with Laura's gun?'

'Didn't I just tell you to shut up?' Meredith's eyes were venomous slits. She stepped closer, brandishing the weapon in Loveday's face.

Loveday put up her hands in a placating gesture. 'OK, Meredith. You're in charge. I'm only asking that you get help for Laura before it's too late.'

Meredith's upper lip curled up in

distaste. 'I'm not helping that bitch. Why should I? She did nothing to help me. This is all her fault. Everything that's happened is her fault.' She paused, blinking rapidly. 'It was her idea to kill Silas, not mine. But I went along with it to please her. She could never have heaved him up that tree by herself.'

Loveday's eyes widened in horror at what she was hearing. Her mind scrolled back to the first time she had met this woman at the Venning house. Meredith had called, supposedly to comfort Laura. The pair of them had spun the story of Silas having been murdered. She couldn't prevent the gasp of realization. It had all been an act — put on for her benefit.

If she'd been near the wall she would have put out a hand to steady herself. She focused on stopping her knees from giving way. This pair had set up the whole thing . . . and they had roped her in to make their story stand up.

Loveday stared at Meredith. 'I've been set up, haven't I? The interview . . . the feature for the magazine . . . it was all part of your and Laura's plan to murder

Silas? You had to get me on board from the start so you could play out your little scene that day, hoping I would tell . . . ' She hesitated. 'Hoping I would repeat what the two of you were saying to Detective Inspector Kitto.'

Meredith gave her a sly smile. 'Laura and I knew all about you and your policeman friend. You don't think we would carry out something like this without doing our homework, do you?'

Loveday met the cold green eyes. 'But it hasn't gone according to plan, has it?' She gave a shrug, hoping she looked more confident than she felt. 'I mean, you weren't expecting me to turn up here. I imagine that kind of throws a spanner in the works for you.'

She shrank back as the woman waved the gun about again, her mouth curving into a sneer. 'No one's indispensable, Miss Ross, not even a magazine editor. I'll not deny that your presence here is a bit of a setback, but I'll deal with that, just as I've done with everything else.'

She glanced to the body on the floor. 'Laura was never as smart as she thought she was. The drugs were a big mistake. I didn't want to get involved in that from the start. It was Laura who insisted we were partners.'

'Drugs?' Loveday's voice came out in a disbelieving squeak. Both women were involved in the Venning Marine drug running? She'd been trying to picture Laura's reaction when she found out about the drugs, and she had been right in the middle of it all along. She would never trust anyone again!

Meredith nodded. She was still keeping a tight hold on the gun. 'But I was wrong. It turned out to be a nice little operation. Laura had contacts. They were organized. The drugs came in from Colombia. They were left in submerged packages at a spot marked by a buoy about thirty kilometres offshore.'

Loveday's eyes were still on the gun. 'Are you telling me that *you* picked up these drugs packages, Meredith?'

'It wasn't always me. I only got involved after that young hothead, Brian Penrose got himself jailed for drunk-driving.' She paused, frowning. 'I think he killed some woman.'

Loveday felt sick. The woman Penrose had killed was Tessa, and now Penrose himself had been killed. Mown down by a hit-and-run driver outside Exeter Prison. Had these two women also been responsible for that?

Meredith was still talking. She actually looked proud of what she had done. She said, 'The pick-ups were arranged to coincide with the sea trials of Silas's yachts. I'm a pretty fair yachtswoman and could handle the new craft. It seemed obvious for me to take over from Penrose.'

'Who killed Brian Penrose?' Loveday asked coldly.

Meredith shrugged. 'Laura handled that.' She gave Loveday a sickly smile. 'She knows people.'

Another horrifying thought struck Loveday. 'What about your Uncle Michael? Whose idea was it to sabotage his car?'

Meredith's eyes flicked down to Laura's motionless body. She'd been suspicious about that accident from the start, which was why she'd made a point of discovering what garage the Jaguar had been taken to for repair. Meredith had paid the place a visit. She'd seen the cut in the brake fluid lead for herself and knew instantly who was responsible.

She waved the gun in the direction of Laura's motionless body. '*She* did that. It was the one thing I couldn't forgive her. She knows how much I care about that old guy, and still she tried to kill him.'

'But why?' Loveday asked.

'Because he ran a better business than she did. My uncle Michael's boatyard was taking business from Venning Marine. Laura couldn't handle that.' She sighed, her eyes still on the woman at her feet.

'What happened?' Loveday asked.

'I came to see her, to accuse her of trying to kill Michael. She didn't deny it. She said she did it for us.' Meredith shook her head. 'You can't imagine how out-raged I was. The woman's not stable. She's dangerous. I had to put a stop to what she was doing. She tried to talk me round . . . lured me down here to the boathouse with some story about evidence we needed to get rid of.'

Meredith sighed heavily. 'Laura said we

had problems over the drugs. The people who picked them up from the yachts had left something behind. Like an idiot, I followed her down here. She had a syringe . . . '

Laura stirred, and made a moaning sound. Meredith flashed her a disgusted look. 'I came round from whatever she had injected into me, and found Laura trying to drag me out onto the boat landing. I suppose the plan was to take me somewhere out to sea and then dump me overboard.' She nodded to a shelf laden with ropes and other sailing paraphernalia. 'There was a torch. I grabbed it and just whacked her hard. She went down like a sack of potatoes.' She swallowed. 'I was finishing tying her up when you came down.'

Loveday was still clinging to the hope that Sam had picked up her call. Was it too much to hope that he was on his way here right now?

'You're not a killer, Meredith.' Loveday tried to reason with her. 'You told me yourself . . . you save people.'

Meredith frowned, staring at her as

though she was a crazy person. 'But that's exactly why I must do what I'm doing. Don't you see? If I let you live, you'll tell the police everything. And if I'm locked up, then I can't save any more patients.' She gave her a hard stare, and Loveday saw the insanity in her eyes. These two women were the same, she realized. They were both mad!

'It's not personal, please don't think that, Loveday. I actually liked you.' Meredith flicked the gun towards Laura. 'Now help me get her into the boat.'

As Meredith bent to grab Laura's shoulders, Loveday saw her chance and made a grab for the gun. It went off with an ear-piercing crack, the bullet ricocheting off the stone wall. Both women flinched. Meredith made a wild swing at Loveday, smashing the barrel of the handgun across her temple. An explosion of red pain shot through Loveday's head . . . and once again, the blackness came down.

23

Loveday was alone in the boathouse when she came to. The place was in total darkness. She could have been out cold for days, for all she knew. How much damage could two blows to the head do to someone's brain? She tried struggling to her feet, but felt so giddy that she was forced to collapse back onto the stone floor. Why had Meredith left her here? Had she believed she was dead? No, she was a doctor. She would have known she was still breathing. There was only one possibility. The woman was coming back to finish her off!

Loveday had to get out of there. Thoughts were swimming around in her head. She tried to remember what had happened to her phone. It wasn't in her pocket. And then she remembered Meredith snatching it away from her when she'd tried to call for help. Was it still on the floor? But where?

She made another attempt to struggle to her feet, but her legs felt like jelly. There was no way she could walk — but she could crawl. She sat for a moment, blinking into the blackness, desperately trying to make sense of where she was. She had no idea how far she was from the stairs, but if she could find her way to the wall, then maybe she could feel her way to them.

On hands and knees she moved slowly, cautiously across the floor, peering into the dark. Her hand touched something wet, and she snatched it back. Was it water? It could have come from the river. But a more chilling thought was seeping into her consciousness. Could it be Laura's blood? Was this where her body had lain, battered and bleeding? Loveday shivered. She could feel hot tears on her cheeks and made an irritated swipe at them. Crying would do her no good. She had to get out of this place.

She tried to think. If this really was the spot where she'd seen Laura's body, then she could work out the location of the stairs. She turned, feeling her way in the dark, making for the back of the boat-house. Inch by inch she covered the floor, reaching out, trying to make sense of each contour she could feel.

And then her hand felt . . . what? Was it a ledge? Was it a step? She felt higher. It was a step . . . and then another. She'd found the stairs!

Cautiously, she began to clamber up. There weren't many steps, twenty at most. But she couldn't see a light at the top. Would the door be locked?

24

The pain of being gun-whipped seared through Loveday's head as she dragged herself up the steps. When she reached the top, she hauled herself to her feet, desperately pulling at the door. It didn't budge. Meredith had locked her in. She sank to her knees, no longer caring how hard she cried. Somewhere at the back of her mind she thought she'd rung Sam for help. Why wasn't he here?

How much longer did she have before Meredith returned to finish the job? In fact, she could hear her now. She could clearly hear footsteps out in the hall. Any minute, she would open the door, and . . .

There was another sound. She listened. The piercing squeals of sirens . . . the screech of tyres . . . and then running feet. She could hear the big police boots pounding all over the house, her name being shouted.

'I'm down here,' she whimpered. 'I'm here, Sam.'

Suddenly the double doors to the boathouse were thrown open, the wood scraping against the stone path outside.

'Loveday! Loveday!' It was Sam's voice.

'I'm here, Sam. I'm on the stairs.'

He was still calling her name. He hadn't heard her. She wished with all her heart that she could fly down those stairs, rush into his arms. But she couldn't move. She was swimming in a sea of darkness and she couldn't escape.

And then suddenly she felt herself being lifted . . . carried off into a vast white space.

'Ambulance. Has that bloody ambulance arrived yet?' The voice was familiar.

Someone was stroking her hair, speaking her name. She tried to open her eyes, but the lids would not move. She tried to smile, but the pain that flashed across her cheeks was too much to bear.

Voices drifted in and out of her consciousness. 'The women have been picked up, sir, on the other side of the river. One of them is in a bad way, but she's alive.'

Women? What women? Her head hurt.

* * *

It was two days later before Loveday eventually surfaced. It was like emerging from a fog. She felt wonderfully, woozily relaxed. Sam was there by her bed, smiling down at her.

'How do you feel?' he asked, his eyes full of concern.

'Like I've been to hell and back.'

He moved a strand of hair gently back from her forehead with a finger. 'You have . . . but you're back now, and I intend keeping you very, very safe from now on.'

Loveday's head sank back into the soft hospital pillow. 'Have I died and gone to heaven, Sam?' She smiled up at him.

'What makes you think you'd get into heaven?' He laughed, his brown eyes twinkling.

'So I'm not dead, then?'

'No, Loveday. You're not dead.' He put his arms around her and whispered playfully in her ear: 'But if you put yourself in danger like that again, I may have to kill you myself.'

*　*　*

It was two days before the doctors would allow Loveday out of bed, but as soon as she was able to move, her first priority was to see Michael Clayton. She shuddered to imagine how distressed he must now be feeling. His beloved niece Meredith, and the woman she had once been so close to, Laura Venning, were both facing murder charges and drug smuggling offences.

Loveday was surprised to find him sitting in a chair by his bed. He had colour in his cheeks and an animated expression on his face as he barked out orders on his mobile phone.

'The Belmont order has to be finished by the end of the week. Don't let them slack, Vincent.

'And what about the SP72? Yes, I know that, but I'm depending on you. We definitely can't afford to run over time on this one.'

He glanced up, saw Loveday standing in the doorway, and waved her in.

'I have to go now, Vincent, but keep me posted.'

He clicked off the call and stood to embrace her.

This wasn't the man she remembered . . . the man who had looked so poorly last time she saw him. Then, he had been pleading with her to find Meredith. The news about her was probably as bad as it could get, and yet Michael Clayton looked happy. What was going on?

'My dear girl. You look like you've been through the wars.'

Loveday touched her bandaged head.

Michael looked shocked. 'Did Meredith do that to you?'

'Not on her own. She and Laura both had a whack at my head.'

He sighed, turning, and sat down heavily in his chair. 'This is all my fault. I asked you to go to Laura's place looking for Meredith. If I'd known . . . '

Loveday put out a hand to reassure him. 'How could you possibly have known what the pair of them had been up to? I'm so sorry, Michael. This must be awful for you.'

'It would have been worse if Meredith had gone missing and I was never to see her again. But yes, she's done a terrible thing. The fact that she seems to have been led on by Laura doesn't absolve her of any blame. I'm just grateful that she's still actually alive.'

Loveday had a dozen questions, but the old man seemed to have found a way of coping with the situation. Maybe Meredith wasn't as bad, or as mad, as Laura, but to Loveday's mind she was not very far off it. However, if her uncle could take comfort from the fact that she was neither dead nor missing, then who was she to question it?

She smiled. 'I just wanted to make sure you were OK, and I can see that you are. I just didn't expect to find you back in the throes of work so soon. You should still be taking things easy,' she scolded.

Michael eyed her with amusement, and Loveday was again aware of the hand-some, engaging man he must have been in his youth. But there was something else, too. Could that be a glint of triumph in the steely blue eyes?

'It's good of you to be concerned about an old codger like me, my dear, but I'll be out of here within the week — and back doing what I do best, which is work.'

Loveday gave a relenting sigh and nodded towards the phone, which was lying on the bed. 'Sounds like there's plenty of work for you back at your yard.' She gave him a sheepish grin. 'Sorry . . . I couldn't help overhearing.'

'We're ticking over.'

'That's more than Venning Marine is doing now.' She had a sudden thought. 'What will happen to the place? I can't imagine it carrying on when the two top people, Silas and Laura, are no longer a part of things.'

'I daresay someone will rescue the company,' Michael said.

Loveday couldn't help noticing the smile as he looked away.

The wheels in her head were whirring again. Had this been part of the plan all along. Was Michael involved in bringing Venning Marine to its knees? But, no, the idea was too far-fetched to even consider. And yet . . .

Loveday was still thinking about this as she went back to her ward, but on seeing Sam waiting by her bed, arms folded, all thoughts of Michael Clayton vanished.

'This is progress.' He smiled, nodding down to her legs as he gathered her into his arms. 'Not overdoing things, are we?'

'No, just practising for when I can get out of here. Fancy taking me for a coffee?'

They took the lift to the hospital's ground floor and found a table in the café. Loveday stirred the latte he'd put in front of her. 'All the loose ends tied up now?' she asked.

Sam nodded. 'More or less. Both women pled guilty to all charges, which makes life simpler for all of us.'

'And the killing of Brian Penrose?'

'Laura Venning admitted arranging that. If he'd been allowed to repeat everything he knew, it would have been like putting a lighted torch under Venning Marine. She couldn't let that happen.'

Loveday screwed up her face. 'But why kill Silas?'

Sam's shoulders lifted into a shrug. 'Who knows? Maybe she just didn't like him taking up with her girlfriend.'

'Or . . .' Loveday said, carefully putting her cup back on its saucer. ' . . . maybe the drugs business wasn't his idea at all. Maybe he was fed up being bossed around by Laura and threatened to pull the plug on her little racket.' She took a sip of coffee. 'Was Meredith involved in killing Silas?'

'According to Laura, she only rang Meredith for help to lift him onto the tree after she'd killed him.'

'And what about Meredith's part in the drug smuggling?'

'She maintains she only did what Laura told her. Laura was the dominant one in the relationship, and Meredith just wasn't strong enough to stand up to her.'

'Is that her defence?' Loveday had to stop her voice from rising. This wasn't the impression she'd got at all when Meredith was pointing the gun at her in the boathouse. If she was remembering right, the woman had also told her she had been very much involved in the drug smuggling, had even taken part in the pick-ups. She'd been confident enough then because she thought Loveday wouldn't be around to tell the tale.

She looked up, meeting Sam's eyes. 'Has Meredith been charged with attempting to murder me?'

'Both women have, but of course they're denying it.'

25

Cassie had nipped into Loveday's cottage and lit the fire, and the flames were flickering cosily up the chimney when Sam brought her home from hospital. A welcoming committee of Cassie, Adam, Sophie and little Leo had met them at the top of the drive, but they had refused to join them in the cottage.

'You two need some quality time together,' Cassie had said, hugging Loveday. 'I'll call by in the morning.'

Loveday could hardly believe she was home. All she wanted to do now was to forget the past couple of weeks, forget the whole Venning family and everybody connected to them. But as they let themselves into the kitchen, the first thing she saw was an enormous, expensive bouquet of flowers.

Loveday shot Sam an excited smile, but he held up his hands. 'They're not from me. There's a card . . . look.'

Loveday extricated the gold-rimmed card from the petals of a rose and read it.

To Loveday, my new friend.
For all you have done for me.
Take care, and keep well.
Michael Clayton

Sam raised an eyebrow. 'What does he mean? What did you do for him?'

Loveday described the scene in Michael Clayton's private hospital room when he'd asked her to go to Laura's house.

'Clayton sent you to the Venning house?' Sam was staring at her. 'You never mentioned that before.'

'I suppose I just forgot. Does it matter?'

'I'm not sure,' he said slowly. He moved into the kitchen, then Loveday could hear him on the phone, talking to Will.

Loveday could feel a chill spreading into her bones, and she wasn't sure why. She only knew she'd felt uneasy that last time she'd talked with Michael Clayton.

It was when she'd mentioned the demise of Venning Marine and asked him what he thought would happen to it now. But, in an instant, she knew the answer. Of course! Michael's company would buy it — and they'd get it at a knock-down price. Had that been at the heart of everything that had happened? A shudder ran through her. Could the whole scenario have been stage-managed by Meredith and her uncle from the very beginning?

It wouldn't have been difficult for Meredith to get inside Laura's head, to control her, to get her to do whatever she suggested. Was it Meredith who had set up the drug-smuggling deal? Had *she* been the one with the contacts, and not Laura, as she had claimed?

Had Meredith suggested Laura should kill Silas? Was it her who had arranged Brian Penrose's killing?

Loveday tried to calm her thoughts. If she was right, it put a completely new light on things. She remembered how keen Michael had been to insist that it had been Laura who forced Meredith to do as she said, but it could just as easily have been the other way round. The more she considered it, the more she was convinced she was right. Meredith had been the villain here all along — but was she in turn being controlled by her uncle?

There would have been a few surprises for them along the way. Loveday didn't think the pair would have expected Laura to sabotage Michael Clayton's car. That must have been quite a setback for both of them.

Sam came back into the room with his brows knitted. 'How well did you know Meredith Deering?' he said.

★ ★ ★

Loveday had asked to be with Sam when he interviewed Michael Clayton in hospital. It was highly irregular, but she knew a more formal interview would take place later. She needed to see his face when he was asked about his part in the Venning Marine case.

He denied everything at first, as they knew he would. But Meredith had been re-interviewed, and had admitted the true version of how things had happened. Once she got talking about the power she could wield over Laura, there was no stopping her.

The seeds of the idea to bring Venning Marine to its knees had come from Michael Clayton. The drugs contacts had been his. It had been Michael who set the whole thing up, aided and abetted by Meredith. But they had very cleverly convinced Laura that the idea was hers, knowing they needed her co-operation to persuade Silas to join her.

Laura was such a volatile character that the pair knew it would only be a matter of time before the whole house of cards that was Venning Marine came tumbling down.

Loveday studied Michael Clayton's face for any sign of remorse — and found none. How could she ever have thought this was a good, kind man? The face she saw now was sneering and arrogant. She tried to meet his eyes, but he looked away, obviously determined to avoid her.

She had so many questions she wanted to fire at him, but Sam had warned her to stay silent. Not that it mattered, because Clayton was saying nothing. He hadn't uttered a word throughout the entire interview.

But Liam Barnes had talked. He had admitted working for Clayton all along. He hadn't been happy about the drugs side of things. He'd told Sam and Will that when they had interviewed him under caution back at the station.

He had been shocked when Silas was killed — and very frightened. He said he had tried to warn the two detectives about what had been going on in the company when they came to Venning Marine that day. That was why he'd told them about the company's financial problems ... that was why he had mentioned Clayton's boatyard. Didn't he deserve some special treatment for being so co-operative?

Sam hadn't been impressed. Barnes may have been a lesser player in the whole dirty business, but he wasn't without guilt. There would be no concessions for the man.

A police guard had been posted on the door to Clayton's private ward, and the officer nodded to Loveday and Sam as they passed him on the way out.

They had just started down the corridor when they heard Clayton calling. They looked at each other, and then waited.

Clayton called again. 'Miss Ross . . . '

Loveday turned, and walked slowly back to the private room Michael Clayton occupied. He looked up when he saw her, still exuding supreme confidence. A chill ran up Loveday's spine.

He smiled. 'I hope you liked the flowers, Miss Ross,' he said.

We do hope that you have enjoyed reading this large print book.

Did you know that all of our titles are available for purchase?

We publish a wide range of high quality large print books including:
Romances, Mysteries, Classics
General Fiction
Non Fiction and Westerns

Special interest titles available in large print are:
The Little Oxford Dictionary
Music Book, Song Book
Hymn Book, Service Book

Also available from us courtesy of Oxford University Press:
Young Readers' Dictionary
(large print edition)
Young Readers' Thesaurus
(large print edition)

For further information or a free brochure, please contact us at:
Ulverscroft Large Print Books Ltd.,
The Green, Bradgate Road, Anstey,
Leicester, LE7 7FU, England.
Tel: (00 44) **0116 236 4325**
Fax: (00 44) **0116 234 0205**

GIRL MEETS BOY

Jack Iams

Reunited with his English war bride, Sybil, after two years, Tim takes her back to the USA with him — but where to live, in the middle of the post-World War II housing crisis? They meet a friend of Sybil's deceased father, who promises to help. Next thing they know, the New Jersey chapter of the British-American War Brides Improvement Association arranges accommodation for them in the isolated coastal community of Merry Point. Here they meet their curmudgeonly landlord and an inept handyman. Then Sybil finds a body on the pier . . .

FIRE IN THE VALLEY

Catriona McCuaig

Spring is just around the corner in Llandyfan, and the first crocuses are beginning to bloom. Then the beautiful morning is shattered by the discovery of a corpse in the glebe — the victim of a grisly murder. Who could have wanted poor Fred Woolton, the mild-mannered milkman, dead? Midwife Maudie once again turns sleuth! Despite expecting a baby of her own, she is not about to take it easy while a case needs to be solved . . .